⚬ THE ⚬ CONQUEST

Julia Templeton

heat | new york

THE BERKLEY PUBLISHING GROUP
Published by the Penguin Group
Penguin Group (USA) Inc.
375 Hudson Street, New York, New York 10014, USA
Penguin Group (Canada), 90 Eglinton Avenue East, Suite 700, Toronto, Ontario M4P 2Y3, Canada
(a division of Pearson Penguin Canada Inc.)
Penguin Books Ltd., 80 Strand, London WC2R 0RL, England
Penguin Group Ireland, 25 St. Stephen's Green, Dublin 2, Ireland (a division of Penguin Books Ltd.)
Penguin Group (Australia), 250 Camberwell Road, Camberwell, Victoria 3124, Australia
(a division of Pearson Australia Group Pty. Ltd.)
Penguin Books India Pvt. Ltd., 11 Community Centre, Panchsheel Park, New Delhi—110 017, India
Penguin Group (NZ), 67 Apollo Drive, Rosedale, North Shore 0632, New Zealand
(a division of Pearson New Zealand Ltd.)
Penguin Books (South Africa) (Pty.) Ltd., 24 Sturdee Avenue, Rosebank, Johannesburg 2196,
South Africa

Penguin Books Ltd., Registered Offices: 80 Strand, London WC2R 0RL, England

This is an original publication of The Berkley Publishing Group.

This is a work of fiction. Names, characters, places, and incidents either are the product of the author's imagination or are used fictitiously, and any resemblance to actual persons, living or dead, business establishments, events, or locales is entirely coincidental. The publisher does not have any control over and does not assume any responsibility for author or third-party websites or their content.

First edition: August 2008

Library of Congress Cataloging-in-Publication Data

Templeton, Julia.
   The conquest / Julia Templeton.—1st ed.
      p.   cm.
   ISBN 978-0-425-22341-3
   1. Highlands (Scotland)—Fiction.   2. Scotland—History—1057–1603—Fiction.   I. Title.
   PS3620.E467C66 2008
   813'.6—dc22

                                                    2008013944

PRINTED IN THE UNITED STATES OF AMERICA

10   9   8   7   6   5   4   3   2   1

Berkley Heat titles by Julia Templeton

THE BARGAIN

RETURN TO ME

THE CONQUEST

To my editor, Leis Pederson,
for her wonderful advice and guidance

ONE

The Highlands of Scotland, 1080

"Rhiannon, do not swim out too far! We cannot be late."

"Quit fretting, Elspeth," Rhiannon replied to her maid, rinsing her hair in the loch's cool water. "Father said supper would be delayed this evening."

Elspeth crossed her arms in a stance Rhiannon knew all too well. Any argument would be futile. "That is true, but do ye not want ample time to prepare for your betrothed's arrival?"

Hearing the word *betrothed* made the hair on the back of Rhiannon's neck stand on end. "To be honest, I do not care what Malgor de Cion thinks of me."

"Ye are far too stubborn for your own good, girl," Elspeth said, shaking out Rhiannon's kirtle and laying it over a large, flat rock. "And it will be me who takes the brunt of your father's anger when ye show up late to meet your betrothed, ill dressed and with your hair soaking wet."

"Perhaps de Cion himself will be so furious, he will call off the wedding." Rhiannon could not keep the hope from her voice.

Elspeth sighed heavily. "Ye have helped make de Cion a wealthy man. Plus, one look at ye, and he will be besotted."

Rhiannon ignored the disturbing words and floated on her back, staring up at the large canopy of trees. Her stomach coiled in distress. Being the only daughter of a chieftain, she knew she would one day be expected to marry. She had just never envisioned herself moving so far away from the only home she had ever known.

Once she left to marry the Norman knight, she would never again see this loch, the trees overhead, or the rolling hills and mountains of her homeland.

"Do ye think England is like Scotland, Elspeth?"

"I do not know. From what I understand, Castle Almeron is on the Scottish border, which makes me believe the two could not be so very different from one another."

"But what if there are differences? What if there are no lochs, no trees, no hills or mountains? No other place could be as beautiful as the Scottish Highlands."

Elspeth approached the loch's edge, the water lapping at her feet. "I think it is safe to say there will be lochs, rivers, and ponds aplenty in England, and trees as well."

"What of the mountains?"

"And mountains, too," the maid said with a soft smile. "Ye shall learn to love our new home just as ye love Castle MacKay. True, it will be hard to leave those that we care for, but we shall manage. I'll never leave ye, Rhiannon. Ye know that."

Rhiannon nodded. "Aye, I know that."

Planting her hands on her curvaceous hips, Elspeth glanced over her shoulder for the third time in as many minutes.

"Who do ye look for?"

"No one," she said, bending over to rinse her hands in the water.

"What if Baron de Cion is ugly?"

Elspeth sighed heavily. "I swear ye are your own worst enemy, Rhiannon."

"What if he is ugly, though?"

"And what if he is handsome?"

"That would be lovely."

The maid grinned.

"But I fear, Elspeth, that he is ugly."

Shaking her head, Elspeth splashed playfully at Rhiannon. "Soon the mystery will be over. Lord Malgor will be here, and ye can ask him all the questions ye have been fretting about for weeks now."

The past months since Rhiannon had learned of her engagement to the newly promoted Lord Malgor, she could think of little else. Was he tall, short, fat, skinny, old, young? Every time she asked her father the simplest of questions, he became agitated with her. Her stepmother, Deirdre, the woman who had stolen her father's heart from her mother, had smiled coyly, no doubt enjoying the fact that Rhiannon would soon be out of their lives forever.

Elspeth paced along the water's edge, her gaze continually drifting toward the trees that surrounded the loch.

Rhiannon swam closer until she could stand in the water, her toes curling into the sand and small rocks beneath her feet. "Who do ye look for, Elspeth?"

"No one," Elspeth replied a touch too quickly.

Scanning the brush, Rhiannon's heart skipped a beat seeing a man in the distance, walking toward them. Though she was well under water, she covered her breasts with her arm. "There is someone in the thicket just over there," she said, pointing in the direction of the intruder.

"Where?" Elspeth's voice held no fear, but rather was tinged with excitement.

"Just there, to the right of the path." Rhiannon squinted against the sun. "It looks like Antony. What on earth is he doing here?"

"I shall be back shortly." Elspeth glanced back at Rhiannon, a sparkle in her eyes that had not been there moments before. "By the time I return, please be dressed and ready."

Rhiannon frowned, confused by her friend's odd behavior. Minutes ago Elspeth had been urging her to get out of the water, and now she was wandering off with the stable master? No wonder she had been acting so strangely all afternoon. She had been planning a tryst.

Scandalous woman.

Antony waved at Rhiannon, a friendly smile on his face. She waved back, and watched as the two walked away, down the pathway, hand in hand.

She hadn't even realized Elspeth liked Antony, aside from friendly greetings whenever they passed by each other in the bailey or the great hall. Apparently things had progressed without Rhiannon even being aware.

But why would she have not said anything about liking Antony? Rhiannon thought back over the weeks and could not recall a single conversation that included the stable master. Sure, there were things one kept to oneself, but had the tables been turned, Rhiannon would have told Elspeth.

In fact, when Rhiannon had become smitten with Gerard, the

goldsmith's grandson who lived in a nearby village, she had told Elspeth that every time she saw the young man, she became weak at the knees.

Did Elspeth not trust her? The very thought made her furious.

She knew enough about love to know what Elspeth and Antony were about. Neither one would be able to slip away at any other time during the day, so they had planned this meeting.

Curious, she swam to shore and, making sure no one was about, rushed from the water and snatched the drying cloth from the rock. If she were discovered spying, she would just have to come up with an excuse, such as she had heard noises and gone to investigate the cause.

With her mind made up, Rhiannon dressed and headed up the pathway, one of many that led back to the castle. The two could not be very far away since Elspeth was supposed to be watching Rhiannon.

Elspeth had always been extremely overprotective where Rhiannon was concerned, and yet she had barely given her a second glance before leaving her alone in the water, and without another soul around.

Rhiannon had walked a fair distance and considered turning around and returning to the loch, when she heard a low-throated moan pierce the quiet.

Her heart rate accelerated and she followed the sound deeper into the thick trees. The closer she came to the sounds, the more nervous she became. She envisioned the two wrapped in a heated embrace, kissing furiously.

Perhaps they were doing more than kissing . . .

She knew she should leave them alone, let them have this rare time together. But no matter how much she tried to convince

5

herself to do just that, her feet would not obey and she continued walking.

Rhiannon's breath caught in her throat seeing Elspeth flat on her back in the soft green grass, and Antony settled between her legs. The maid's soft blonde curls had fallen out of her sloppy bun and now spread out about her in tangled disarray. Her gown had crept up, or perhaps had been tossed up about her waist, her naked thighs spread wide. The stable master still wore a tunic, but his braies were bunched down past his knees, his buttocks bare, the muscle flexing there as he cupped his hips.

A wave of heat rolled through Rhiannon as she watched the young lovers kiss. Elspeth's fingers slid into Antony's hair as he cupped one small breast, his thumb brushing over an extended nipple. His mouth left Elspeth's. He kissed a path down the side of her neck, to the pulse beating wildly there, before continuing to her chest, where he tasted a nipple. His tongue danced around the bud before covering it again with his lips.

Rhiannon's nipples tightened as she watched the young man pleasure her friend, and an unfamiliar heat rushed to her groin, and between her thighs.

Elspeth moaned low in her throat, almost desperately, her head moving from side to side in the soft grass as Antony played homage to one breast and then the other. "That feels so good," she said in a voice Rhiannon hardly recognized.

Antony took one of Elspeth's hands and brought it down to his sex. "Feel what ye do to me."

Elspeth smiled as her fingers wrapped around Antony's thick cock. "Already hard as stone."

"Aye, lass. Your touch makes me that way."

She gripped him firmly, her hand moving up and down in a

practiced rhythm that had Antony groaning, his breathing shallow, his hips thrusting in time with her movements.

"God's breath, I need ye," he said almost desperately, using his knees to spread her thighs wider. "Ye have no idea how long I have yearned to be with ye, Elspeth. This is like a dream."

Elspeth laughed softly, and pulled him down for a kiss, her mouth moving over his ravenously.

I shall stay for just a moment more, and then leave them alone.

Elspeth licked her lips and watched her lover with longing. "No more talking, Antony. I want ye now." She guided his rigid cock inside her. As he thrust home, she moaned loudly, the sound sending birds flying from their nests.

The two lovers didn't even hear; they were too lost in their own world.

Rhiannon pressed tight against a tree, her fingers digging into the bark. Her entire body burned with a need that scared her, and yet strangely fascinated her. How would it feel to be in Elspeth's place? To have a man moving over her, inside her, his thick length stretching her, thrusting in and out, in and out, while telling her how much he desired her.

A soft cry escaped Elspeth's lips and her eyes closed as she lifted her hips to meet each solid stroke, the expression on her face one of pure rapture.

Antony kissed her, and she opened her mouth to receive him, their tongues mating furiously. Rhiannon touched her lips, wondering and yearning for such a kiss.

Soon she would be married and her husband would expect her to do the same. A man she knew absolutely nothing about, save for the fact he was a French soldier who had come to England with King William, and had been given her hand and extensive dowry for his service to his king. It was a marriage that would help ease the rift between England and Scotland, her father had said.

But what of her heart? She would never experience what these two lovers shared. True desire for each other. A need brought on by attraction and friendship.

Antony stopped moving his hips as he laved one nipple, then the other, his tongue flicking wildly over and around.

With a frustrated moan, Elspeth arched against him, almost desperately, and yet he did not move. "Fuck me," she finally said, the words so unexpected Rhiannon's eyes rounded to hear such language coming from her maid.

Finally, Antony looked up at Elspeth, a soft, albeit surprised smile on his lips. "I hear ye, lass." He slid in and out of her, inching the maid across the soft grass with each hard thrust. "I love ye, Elspeth."

Rhiannon's heart skipped a beat. She did not realize her best friend was in love, and wondered again why Elspeth had not confided in her.

"That feels nice," Elspeth replied, saying nothing of love or the declaration Antony had just made.

His brows furrowed for a minute until she whispered, "Ye are so big, Antony. So thick. Ye make me mad with desire."

The frown dissipated. He pumped against her in deep, even thrusts, the fierce movements making her breasts bounce. "And ye are so hot and tight, lass. So sweet."

Elspeth grabbed his buttocks with both hands, squeezing hard, her legs wrapping around his waist.

"Ye like that, don't ye?" Antony's face looked strained.

"Aye, I do."

Rhiannon's gaze shifted down the man's body, where he joined with Elspeth. Her pulse quickened seeing his long, slick cock enter and retreat into the maid.

The flesh between her legs tingled, growing damp.

"Are ye comin', lass?" Antony asked in a deep, husky voice.

Coming where? Rhiannon thought to herself as Elspeth's hands moved up his back to cling to his shoulders, her nails biting into his skin.

Rhiannon shifted. A twig snapped beneath her feet and Antony stopped for a moment, glancing over his shoulder. She would be horrified if they discovered her spying on them in such an intimate moment. Holding her breath, she pressed against the tree's large trunk.

"It is nothing." Elspeth reached up, drawing his attention back to her.

To Rhiannon's great relief, the sighs and moans continued, growing in intensity as the slapping of skin against skin quickened.

Daring to breathe again, Rhiannon pushed away from the tree, rushing back to the pathway. She raced toward the loch, pulling her kirtle off as she went. It must appear as though she had just left the water.

She had scarcely caught her breath when Elspeth's laughter came from nearby. Rhiannon pretended to be drying off just as the maid stepped from the trees.

"There ye are," Rhiannon said, hoping Elspeth did not notice she was winded. "I was ready to call out to ye."

"I did not mean to take so long," Elspeth said, a huge smile on her face as she hurried toward Rhiannon. "Antony needed help finding a special herb that grows in the thicket."

Rhiannon almost sighed with relief. "And did ye find what ye needed?"

"Aye, I did," Elspeth responded, her cheeks a rosy pink, her blue eyes bright. When she started humming a merry tune, Rhiannon could not help but smile.

Mayhap marriage would not be so horrible, after all. But then again, what if her husband was not as pleasing as Antony or Gerard, the goldsmith's grandson? Could she do what she had just witnessed with an old man? "I wonder if Lord Malgor will have a pleasing body."

Elspeth frowned. "Most soldiers have pleasing bodies, so I am certain Lord Malgor is no different."

"How do ye know most soldiers have pleasing bodies?"

"They must be in prime condition, the warriors that they are."

"What if de Cion is not handsome, Elspeth? Ye know I cannot hide what I feel. My face has a mind of its own, and if I am disappointed, I am sure to show it."

"Do not fret, lass. For all ye know, he could be the man of your dreams. Mayhap he is tall, handsome, and has a body sure to please."

"With my luck, he will be a toad. An old, tired, ugly, fat toad."

Elspeth cupped Rhiannon's cheek. "And perhaps within lies the heart of a gentleman and truly caring husband who wishes nothing but to please ye. Ye are a strong woman, Rhiannon. Do not ever forget it. If your betrothed is not to your liking, then ye shall find other ways to please yourself. Trust me in this."

"Please myself. In what ways?"

Tilting her head to the side, Elspeth asked, "Have ye no idea what it means to pleasure one's self?"

"I have touched my breasts before, but I doubt that will ever take the place of what happens between a man and a woman."

Elspeth's lips curved in a secret smile that made Rhiannon feel very young. "True, one's own hand cannot make up for the absence of a lover's touch, but if your marriage with de Cion is disappointing or lacking, there are ways to ease the ache in your body. In the days before your wedding we shall discuss how, but for now we must return to the castle and meet your betrothed. Who knows, my dear, perhaps there shall be no need for such a discussion."

"What if he is disappointed when he sees me?"

Elspeth snorted. "Rhiannon, most any woman would give their soul to have your beauty. Your hair is like silk, and your eyes are so unique."

"I was once called a witch because of my eyes."

"Your eyes are unusual because one seldom sees such a color. Ye are an unrivaled beauty and ye shall make your future husband weak at the knees, this I promise."

Some of the trepidation she'd been feeling left her. "What if he is displeased with me in the bedchamber?"

Elspeth closed her eyes and muttered something unintelligible under her breath. "Ye will drive us both crazy if ye do not quit fretting about such things, Rhiannon. Soon ye shall meet your intended and the mystery will be over. And remember, any woman would love to trade places with ye, even if her intended looks like a toad."

"My mother was beautiful and yet my father locked her away," Rhiannon said absently, stepping into her shoes.

"Aye, I have heard the stories, lass."

"How could he vow to love and protect her and yet imprison her? She did nothing to deserve such a fate—save for the fact he loved another. That is why she died so soon, Elspeth. At the time it happened, I was too young to understand the truth. When Father took Deirdre as his bride months later, my heart turned to stone, and I never trusted him again."

As usual, whenever Rhiannon thought of her mother, a mixture of melancholy and anger washed over her. Her mother had been such a docile creature who had loved her husband, and in return had endured horrible atrocities at his hands. And all because *he* had fallen in love with another woman. And now her father would force Rhiannon into an unwanted marriage.

Oh, the irony.

"Do not fret about the things ye cannot change, Rhiannon. If ye are at peace with yourself, then all else will fall into place." Elspeth gathered up the drying cloth and soap. "Come, we have dallied long enough, my dear."

"Promise me this, Elspeth. If de Cion is deplorable, and I have no desire to marry him, will ye flee with me?"

Elspeth took Rhiannon's hand in her own. "Of course. Ye have been like my own daughter, even though ye are but seven years younger than me. I'll never leave ye. Not ever. If ye take one look at de Cion and feel he is not the one for ye, then by God, we shall run as fast and as far as our feet will carry us."

Touched by her friend's devotion, Rhiannon embraced her tightly and kissed her cheek. "Thank ye for leaving everything behind to go with me. I know it must be hard, especially leaving someone ye love."

Putting her at arm's length, Elspeth frowned. "I love no one but my family and ye."

"No one else?"

"Aye, no one."

Rhiannon opened her mouth to ask about Antony when a bell sounded in the distance, making her heart jolt in trepidation.

Elspeth's eyes widened. "Dear God, your betrothed has arrived!"

TWO

Adelstan Cawdor followed Laird MacKay beneath the giant portcullis of Castle MacKay. The immense wooden fortress with a large stone tower sat high on a hill overlooking the coastline, a formidable stronghold that had spent the better part of a century defending itself against the Danes.

A good thing he had come as a guest.

Indeed, he had received a most warm, if not exuberant, reception. Laird MacKay had personally ridden out to meet Adelstan and his men, a wide smile on his face as he bade them welcome. However, that same smile thinned considerably the moment he learned Adelstan had come in place of Malgor de Cion, his daughter's intended.

Laird MacKay's dark eyes narrowed. "Might I assume Lord Malgor is on his deathbed?" There was no misinterpreting the anger in the chieftain's voice.

"*Nearly* on his deathbed," Adelstan said with a reassuring smile he hoped put the older man's fears to rest.

"And what, pray tell, has caused him to be so ill that he could not claim my daughter, his betrothed, himself?"

Adelstan, knowing full well the question would be asked, replied, "He aggravated an old hunting wound on the eve before our departure. The healer insisted he stay behind. Knowing you were expecting him, and not wanting to delay the wedding, I was sent in his stead." Whispers among the ranks said the "wound" came by way of a dagger and a disagreement over a game of chess. De Cion's temper was legendary but had grown more explosive in recent weeks. Many wondered, including their liege, if perhaps his upcoming marriage had been part of the cause. Everyone at Braemere Castle knew de Cion loved his leman, a woman who had been devoted to him for the eleven years since his wife had died in childbirth.

However, the woman had been a commoner and could do nothing to bolster his aspirations or career. She had not taken the news of his upcoming wedding lightly. Renaud de Wulf, their liege and Adelstan's brother-in-law, had suggested Malgor send the woman away, back to her family near London, so that he could start fresh with his new bride and new fief. Castle Almeron was nowhere near as impressive as Braemere, but still brought with it a title and riches, and the opportunity to start a new life with a young bride.

"Ah, a hunting wound," MacKay said, giving away nothing of his thoughts as they continued into the large bailey, where a crowd watched from a distance. "He must trust ye immensely to send ye in his place."

Adelstan nodded. "Actually, it was my liege, Lord de Wulf,

who sent me in de Cion's stead. I assure you, Laird MacKay, your daughter is in capable hands. I will let no harm come to her."

The chieftain stopped and turned to Adelstan, his eyes searching his so intently as to be uncomfortable. A moment later his lips curved slightly. "Ye are a man of your word, Sir Adelstan. My Rhiannon can be a handful, and at times is a bit outspoken and strong-willed for her own good. I hope ye have patience, because ye may need it."

Adelstan was instantly reminded of his sister, Aleysia, who shared similar traits. "Aye, I am a patient man." He noted Lady Rhiannon was not present and wondered at the reason. Did this strong-willed young woman have reservations against marrying de Cion? Mayhap she had heard of the newly titled baron's age and resisted the idea of marrying a much older man.

The Scot stroked his beard. "I think ye and my daughter shall get on very well, Sir Adelstan."

"I am sure we will," Adelstan assured him.

"There should be ample room for your men in the armory." MacKay pointed toward a large wooden building across the bailey. "A guest chamber has been made up in the tower, and ye are welcome to make use of it."

"While I appreciate the offer of a private bedchamber, I assure you it is not necessary. I am content to sleep wherever my men are stationed."

"Ye are here in Lord Malgor's stead, and therefore ye will be treated as he would be treated." His tone let Adelstan know he would accept no refusal.

Adelstan nodded in acquiescence. "Very well. Thank you, Laird MacKay."

"Good, now that is settled, let us get on with the feasting. I am certain ye are all hungry from your long journey. Let us dine and enjoy the entertainment we have in store for this evening."

After he'd lived on dried meat, fruit, and cheese for the past week, Adelstan's stomach rumbled at the thought of filling his belly.

They approached the great hall, where armed guards stood at attention. With intense fanfare they opened the double doors, and a room full of men, women, and children, all dressed in their best, came to their feet.

Applause broke out over the assemblage, growing with intensity as they made their way to the high dais.

How disappointed they would be when they learned he was not Lord Malgor.

"Impressive," Jorden, his next in command, said under his breath, bending his head back to look at the high-timbered ceilings overhead.

Adelstan followed his officer's gaze. "Indeed, the craftsmanship is exceptional."

"Perhaps one day we shall both have fiefs as fine as this one."

Laird MacKay, obviously pleased by Jorden's compliment, genuinely smiled for the first time since Adelstan and his men had arrived. Jorden was a master at charming anyone, both men and women. His silver tongue had gotten them out of more than one scrape. Adelstan's foot soldiers broke away, led by Jorden, who sat at one of the lower tables near the high dais.

When the day came that Adelstan was awarded his own fief, Jorden would be his trusted sergeant-at-arms, and he would take his place at the high table, too.

On the dais, Laird MacKay took a seat in a large chair, and directed Adelstan to take the seat to his right. A woman with long auburn hair approached the table, staring at Adelstan with obvious interest.

Adelstan tried to hide his surprise. Surely this could not be Rhiannon? The woman had to be at least Adelstan's age, and he was just shy of his thirtieth year.

"Sergeant, please meet my wife, Lady MacKay."

Adelstan nodded. "A pleasure to make your acquaintance, Lady MacKay."

She sat and lifted a jewel-encrusted goblet to her lips, watching Adelstan all the while. Either the woman hid her age well, or she was not Rhiannon's birth mother.

Laird MacKay lifted a brow, and placed a hand on his wife's thigh.

Lady MacKay set the goblet down, leaned toward her husband, and whispered something in his ear, her large breasts pressing against his beefy arm.

Adelstan turned his attention away from the couple to the doorway, wondering where Lady Rhiannon was, and if she was going to make an appearance tonight. A sense of foreboding filled the air, making him unsettled.

A servant approached with warm water. Adelstan glanced at the woman, whose cheeks were flushed a soft pink and grew a shade darker the longer he stared. She gently washed the dirt from his hands, her fingers gentle, taking her time. He guessed her to be younger than himself. Wearing her dark hair up in a tidy bun, she had rough hands that bespoke a life of hard work, the nails cut to the quick, her palms deeply calloused.

In recent years he had gained a greater appreciation for servants and the long, arduous tasks they performed each day. Having been born to Saxon royalty and thereby brought up in a wealthy household,

Adelstan had taken those hardworking individuals for granted, until his life had changed so drastically as a young man when King William had stripped his family of their lands and titles.

The woman patted his hands dry, taking far longer than necessary, but he did not mind. In fact, he yearned to ask her to meet him later, to ease the ache in his loins, but would not do so in front of his guest. "Thank you," he said, and she glanced up, her dark gaze falling away almost immediately, but not before he recognized the desire there.

"Forgive my daughter for her tardiness," Laird MacKay said, lifting a handsomely engraved goblet to his lips and taking a long drink. "I am certain it stems from her nervousness at meeting ye, or rather, at meeting her betrothed."

"That, or she is out swimming again," Lady MacKay said, her tone full of exasperation.

A young boy approached the dais steps, and instantly Adelstan recognized Laird MacKay's features and Lady MacKay's eyes. The lad slid into the seat beside his mother, sighed heavily, and immediately started tapping his nails on the table.

Adelstan was surprised when both father and mother ignored him, doing nothing to reprimand the boy.

"Father, forgive me for having arrived late."

Adelstan looked up at a young woman with blue, or rather violet eyes—and his insides coiled. Sweet Jesus, but Rhiannon MacKay was an alluring, exotic creature with long, light brown hair with touches of blonde that fell down her back in thick, soft waves. She wore a kirtle of pale blue linen, which molded nicely to her full, firm breasts and slender waist, and a simple leather girdle accented her slender hips.

Malgor de Cion was a lucky man.

"There ye are, my dear," Laird MacKay said, standing, and Adelstan followed suit.

He bowed. "Lady Rhiannon, it is a pleasure to meet you."

Rhiannon MacKay looked at Adelstan fully, her gaze shifting from his, down his body and slowly back up again. She could disarm a man with such a look. Indeed, all thought slipped away for a moment as he stared into her remarkable eyes.

"Thank ye. How was your journey?" Her lips curved into a warm smile, displaying small, straight white teeth. Warmth spread through his veins, straight to his already rigid cock. She was perfection. An unrivaled prize that men would be talking about for decades to come.

"Very well, thank you," he said, all the while thinking this lovely creature could have been his betrothed. He'd been a high-ranking soldier in his liege's army for as long as Malgor. Ironically, when the fief of Almeron had been offered to one of Renaud's men, Adelstan had bowed out of the running only because de Cion was getting older and had been yearning to become a father since losing his wife and child.

"I have been most anxious to meet ye."

Her Scottish accent flowed over him like warm honey, making him forget for a moment that she believed him to be her betrothed. Before he could remedy the situation himself, her father cleared his throat.

"Daughter, I fear Lord Malgor was unable to make the journey himself. But in his stead, Baron de Wulf has sent his most trusted officer, Adelstan Cawdor, to escort ye to Almeron."

Rhiannon's smile slipped for an instant but she caught herself.

Although her grin returned in force, he recognized disappointment in those incredible eyes, and felt a moment of deep regret.

Intense, bone-jarring regret.

A beauty such as Rhiannon MacKay came around only once in a lifetime and well he knew it. And she would be handed to Malgor de Cion, a man three times her age who, despite having a young woman to wed, would no doubt keep his leman nearby.

Or perhaps the new baron would become so enamored with his new bride, so deeply in love, that he would do the right thing and send his leman away. Adelstan's sister had been fortunate in finding a love match with her enemy, Renaud de Wulf, but their story was a rarity in feudal England.

Adelstan cleared his throat. "Lady Rhiannon, I would like to extend Lord Malgor's apology that he could not come to claim you himself. My liege, Lord Renaud of Braemere, has sent me on your betrothed's behalf. I take my duty seriously and will deliver you safely to Castle Almeron, where Lord Malgor will be awaiting you."

"Why did he not make the journey himself?" she asked, her gaze shifting over him in a way that had him wondering at her innocence. She did not look at him as a virgin would.

"He aggravated an old injury while hunting, and the healer told him it would not be wise to travel."

Alarm came over her fragile features. "An injury?"

"Aye, Lady Rhiannon. The wound is not life-threatening, but serious enough that he could not travel such a distance."

Her full lips quirked, and he was reminded yet again of her father's remarks. "Mayhap he should have waited to make the journey until he was mended."

"Daughter . . ." MacKay said, his voice firm and resolute as he sat.

Rhiannon took a deep breath, her chest rising and falling, and Adelstan's gaze shifted to her full, firm breasts. The kirtle had been embroidered at the neck, a delicate design of silver thread, which continued down, nearly between the luscious globes. He found himself wondering if her nipples would be pale rose or a darker hue. Someone at his officers' table, no doubt Jorden, cleared his throat, and his gaze ripped back to her face. Just in time, too, since her father gave them his full attention.

He most certainly needed to find the servant who had washed his hands moments ago. Perhaps burying his cock deep into another woman would wipe away his traitorous thoughts.

Everything about Rhiannon's features was fragile . . . from the sharp cheekbones, to the tiny tipped-up nose, to the luscious lips, the top curving upward. Such a full mouth, perfect for sucking and licking—

He shook away the thought.

In truth, he wished Rhiannon MacKay were homely instead of breathtakingly beautiful. Though he respected Malgor, he could not for a second envision this lovely young woman with the gruff, middle-aged warrior.

"Daughter, please sit," Laird MacKay said, annoyance in his tone. "Supper is being served."

"May I sit beside ye, Adelstan?" she asked, already sliding onto the bench beside him.

"Of course," he replied, taking his seat.

Rhiannon sat so close to him, their thighs touched. His heart nearly pounded out of his chest.

Adelstan shifted a little, easing some of the contact, but she made no effort to move away. Indeed, she almost looked comfortable as she glanced up at him with those long-lashed eyes, her feminine scent surrounding him, pulling him into her web.

His cock strained against his belly, and he was tempted to excuse himself for a while in order to ease the ache.

And to think it was his duty to bring this strikingly beautiful woman across Scotland to her betrothed. How in God's name would he manage such a feat without touching her?

His liege had told Adelstan to stay at Castle MacKay for as long as Rhiannon needed—within reason—adding that delaying the journey would also give Malgor time to recover from his wound.

"You stare, sir," she said, her full lips splitting into a soft smile. "Do ye find me displeasing?"

He had not realized he'd been staring.

"Forgive me, I did not mean to offend you, and nay, I do not at all find you displeasing, Lady Rhiannon. It's just that I have never before seen eyes such as yours. They're extraordinary."

A soft blush touched her cheeks. She leaned into him, keeping her voice low. "I was once accused of having the eyes of a witch."

He frowned, wondering how anyone could be so cruel. He was ready to say as much when the same servant who had washed his hands moments before now poured wine into his goblet and then into Rhiannon's. The servant stared at Adelstan, her dark eyes telling him she would not deny him.

Her lips curved slightly as their eyes met and held.

Lord knew he could use a tumble this night.

Taking a long drink, he savored the warm effects of the wine and chanced a lingering glance at the servant's backside. It was then he noticed Rhiannon watching him. Did she guess what was on his mind?

The knowing smirk on her lips answered that question.

He looked down at the lower tables, where his men sat, and noticed every single one was staring at Rhiannon, a woman they had sworn to protect. By their pleased expressions, it was obvious they, too, had not expected her to be such a beauty.

Jorden caught his gaze and grinned with open approval. In Adelstan's mind, the smile was altogether too cocky and smug.

Rhiannon toyed with her necklace, a lovely silver cross in the Celtic design. Seeing where his gaze was directed, she smiled.

"Forgive me for staring. I meant no dis—"

"'Tis lovely, is it not?" Her sweet grin instantly put him at ease. "'Twas my mother's, a gift from her parents upon her marriage to my father. I have worn it since her death. It gives me peace and makes me feel a part of her still." She dropped her gaze. "Do ye think me silly?"

"Nay, not at all. It is lovely."

As are you.

"Tell me, Adelstan, was your journey uneventful?"

"Aye, save for the foul weather when we came upon the High-lands."

She laughed lightly, the sound pleasant, touching him in a way that surprised him. "Spoken like a true Englishman."

"I'll have you know, I lived in Scotland for three years."

"Did ye?" she asked, her violet eyes brightening, her white teeth flashing. "Where?"

"Near Loch Linhee."

Her brows furrowed a little, and it did nothing to take away from her beauty. "I do not know of it."

"Do you not? It's but two days' ride south of here. We will ride past it on our way to Almeron. I shall show it to you, if you'd like."

Her eyes had changed the moment he mentioned Almeron and he sensed her sadness. "Lady Rhiannon, I know you must be disappointed Lord Malgor could not make the journey himself, and for that I am truly sorry."

She reached out and touched his hand, her elegant fingers curling around his. He was shocked at the sensation that rushed through him at the casual contact. "My circumstances are not your fault, Adelstan. I trust ye will deliver me safely to my intended."

His instinct was to pull away from her touch, especially when in a room full of people, his own men included. She meant only to comfort him, but that touch rocked him to the core.

She had no idea of the lascivious thoughts racing through his head. The way his cock strained against his braies, or how his blood coursed hot and thick through his veins as he wondered what she looked like beneath that lovely gown.

Realizing he had not responded, he cleared his throat. "I appreciate your vote of confidence, Lady Rhiannon. I shall not let you down."

CHREE

Rhiannon hoped she hid her disappointment well.

When she had entered the great hall and seen the tall, handsome, blond-haired knight at her father's side, her heart rate had increased with each step that brought her closer to him.

God had truly blessed her, she had thought, a mixture of excitement and desire boiling within her. How beautiful he was with his light green eyes framed by long, dark lashes, a straight, perfectly proportioned nose, and sharp cheekbones. In truth, when her gaze locked with his, she had silently thanked her father for accepting the baron's offer in marriage.

Oh, the wicked things they could do together, she and this handsome knight. Things that would make even the saucy Elspeth blush.

Her nipples pebbled against the soft linen of her chemise and kirtle, and a strange tingling started between her thighs.

Perhaps she would not wait until her wedding night to make love to him. Show him how very eager she was to be his woman in every way.

Aye, if he had been her intended, she would do just that.

But Adelstan Cawdor was not her betrothed.

Cruel, cruel world.

Beneath the table she had touched his hand, her fingers sliding over his. She could tell by his body language he was shocked by her actions . . . and yet he did not pull away.

She smiled inwardly. Perhaps the attraction went both ways?

"Adelstan, mayhap ye can tell Rhiannon something of her intended?" her father said, breaking into her wicked thoughts.

Rhiannon dropped her hand to her side, conscious of her father's assessing stare. Was she being *that* obvious?

Adelstan pursed his full lips and Rhiannon wondered what his kisses would taste like. Oh, but he was so handsome. "Certainly, though I know not where to begin."

"How long have ye known Lord Malgor?" Rhiannon asked, drawing his attention back to her. The warmth in those green eyes sent a rush of exhilaration through her.

He ran his tongue along his bottom lip and she stared at the moisture there, resisting the urge to capture his mouth with her own.

As though reading her mind, he cleared his throat. "Lord Malgor has been in service to our liege, Lord Renaud at Braemere, for over a decade. It is his skill and devotion that have gained him the fief of Castle Almeron and your hand."

"I understand Castle Almeron is in the process of being built?" her father asked.

"Aye, it is nearly complete. The keep has been built upon an old Roman ruin and encompasses a large part of a rolling hillside."

"Is there water nearby?" Rhiannon asked absently.

Adelstan smiled then, a boyish grin she felt all the way to her toes.

"Aye, a river flows by the castle, Lady Rhiannon."

She would have preferred a loch, or as the English called it, a lake, but a river would do.

"How old is Lord Malgor?"

"Rhiannon!" her father said, his voice full of exasperation.

"Six and fifty, I believe," Adelstan said, his gaze intent as though gauging her reaction.

Six and fifty! Disappointment twisted in her belly. She had hoped for a younger man, someone closer to her own age.

Her spirits plummeted by the second. She was to marry an old man instead of a virile young warrior like the one sitting at her side. Her shock must have shown on her face, for Adelstan's smile faltered, and she could even see a touch of sympathy in his beautiful green eyes.

She forced a smile, even though she felt like crying. The last thing she wanted was to marry a man older than her father. Nay, she wanted a young, virile man like Adelstan. A man who would make the blood boil within her veins—and make her yearn for all they could experience together, especially in the bedchamber.

Furious, Rhiannon turned to her father. "Did ye hear that, Father, my husband shall be older than ye."

Her father's face fell, and she stared at him for a long moment, refusing to drop her gaze. There were deep lines bracketing his mouth and eyes, and a permanent furrow between his brows.

Would Malgor's stomach also protrude well past his belt, and did he have thinning hair, or mayhap he was bald already?

She felt nauseous, the scent of mutton and cabbage making her stomach curl to her throat.

"Lord Malgor is an honorable man, Lady Rhiannon, and he is delighted you will be his wife," Adelstan said, as though that would help her volatile emotions.

She didn't have to look at her father to know he yearned to reach over and choke her.

Rhiannon picked up a grape and rolled it between her fingers, her gaze shifting around the hall. From the corner of her eye she could feel Adelstan watching her.

"Sir Adelstan, I do not detect a French accent," her stepmother said, and the knight nodded.

"Aye, my lady, I am English. My father was a Saxon Earl, and Braemere Castle was our keep in the north of England."

So he had been royalty . . . until King William had come. Rhiannon was not at all surprised. He had a noble presence. "It must have been difficult to watch your birthright go to another."

He nodded. "It was. My parents were killed, and my sister and I were forced to flee to Scotland."

"I am sorry, Adelstan," Rhiannon said, touching his hand again, but this time briefly.

"As am I," Deirdre said, a soft smile on her face as she watched Adelstan.

Rhiannon recognized the look. Her stepmother desired the English knight.

"I know how difficult it is to lose a parent, and to lose both must have been horrific," Rhiannon said, folding her hands in her lap. "Was it Lord de Wulf who killed—"

"Rhiannon, 'tis a rude question." Deirdre shook her head in exasperation.

"Nay, it is a legitimate question. It was not my liege, but another who killed my parents. A cruel, pompous man who cared little of the innocent lives he took. My only regret is having waited three years to kill him." A nerve in his jaw pulsed.

"*Ye* killed him?"

A darkness came over his face, along with an untouchable pain that had her yearning to throw her arms around him and hold him tight. "Aye, I did."

"So that is how ye came to live in Scotland?"

"Aye."

"Will ye be living at Castle Almeron?" Deirdre asked, obviously working very hard to stay involved in the conversation. Rhiannon could sense her father's agitation.

"Nay. My home is at Braemere—until I take a wife and gain my own fief."

Rhiannon's stomach dropped. "And shall ye marry soon, do ye think?"

"God's breath, Rhiannon, will ye ever learn to hold your tongue? Ye have no right to ask such questions." Her father looked to Adelstan. "Forgive my daughter for her impudence. As I mentioned earlier, she has little trouble speaking her mind."

Heat raced up her neck to her cheeks. How dare her father talk about her as though she were not present? Though she wanted desperately to snap back, she knew her father's temper too well. He was not opposed to slapping her across the face, and had done so a time or two, but never in front of others.

Rhiannon reached for another grape and popped it in her

mouth, chewing slowly, looking at the group of English soldiers who all watched her. One bold officer met her gaze.

As dark as Adelstan was light, the man exuded a confidence that was appealing, as well as a tad unnerving. They had brought a surprisingly small number of men with them, which told her one of two things . . . they were not overly concerned about her safety, or they were extremely skilled warriors.

She guessed it had to be the latter.

At the table behind the English officers, she noted a handsome woman with long, dark hair watching Adelstan intently. Indeed, as Rhiannon looked about, she saw that he had gained the attention of the majority of the women in the hall, which had to be the case everywhere he went. His beauty was a rarity, and she wondered if he had a woman waiting for him back at Braemere.

Her father had become still for the moment, obviously worried about his wife's wandering eye, and an awkward silence followed.

Adelstan ate the venison with graceful fingers. His hands were large, and he wore no rings on his long fingers, but he did have a leather bracelet around his right wrist. Was it a gift from someone? A lover, perhaps? She wanted very much to reach out and touch it, but did not do so, knowing her father would likely come out of his skin.

"Since my betrothed is of advancing years, has he been married before?" Rhiannon asked Adelstan, making sure to keep her voice low so that the others could not hear.

Adelstan nodded. "Aye, he had a wife but she died many years ago."

"How did she die?"

"Childbirth."

Rhiannon swallowed hard and reached for her goblet.

"My sister has given birth four times, and all without difficulty."

"She sounds like a strong woman."

"Aye, she is." There was no mistaking the pride in his voice, or in his expression. "I think the two of you will get on very well."

"I hope to get the chance to meet her."

"You shall. She and her husband will be attending your wedding."

"I am happy to hear that," she said with forced enthusiasm.

Machara, a servant, approached and filled their cups. Rhiannon noted the way she lingered in front of Adelstan, moving the trencher a little, and his plate as well.

Could the woman be any more obvious?

Rhiannon gave up on eating altogether and instead nursed her wine, enjoying its warming effects. It helped to soothe her tattered nerves and ease the strange jealousy when Machara returned to clear the table and proceeded to clean Adelstan's hands as though he were a child.

Adelstan smiled at the woman, his gaze shifting over her.

He wanted Machara? Her gut twisted painfully.

As the tables below were moved to make room for dancing, Rhiannon could not help but think of Malgor, and wondered if he would even dance. Most of the older men, like her father, usually watched everyone else dance from their seats while they drank and conversed. Even now, it was the younger soldiers and women who took to the floor.

Rhiannon's mother had loved to dance and had passed along that love to her.

"Mayhap ye would like to dance with Rhiannon, Sir Adelstan?" her father said, surprising her. No doubt he did so to make up for the fact she had grown silent as supper had progressed.

"Of course." Adelstan turned to her. "It would be my honor."

Rhiannon stood, took his hand, and wrapped her fingers around his long ones. His calloused palm pressed against hers, no doubt hardened by long hours holding weapon and shield. The hands of a warrior. Oh, but to feel those rough hands on her body, touching her in places that even now grew hot and wet with a need that shocked her.

"I hope my dancing does not disappoint, Lady Rhiannon," he said with an apologetic smile. "I admit that I am sorely out of practice."

"Ye would never disappoint me, Adelstan. And please, when we are alone, I should like ye to call me Rhiannon. After all, we are friends, are we not?" Her thumb brushed against his.

His smile faltered as he looked at where their hands touched. Did he think her actions bold and unladylike? Did he guess that she wanted him?

She smiled up at him, dropping his hand as they parted ways and took their places in line with the other dancers. Her heart pounded hard as she stared at him, and he her, while waiting for the music to begin.

How she wished she could read his thoughts and know what he felt when he looked at her. When they had first met, he had commented about her unusual eyes and she had sensed an attraction. But perhaps he was one of those charming men who knew how to say the right thing and look at a woman just so.

Elspeth had once said that all a man must do is look at her a certain way and she knew he wanted to make love to her. Rhiannon had recognized such a look from Gerard every time she saw him at market, but what of Adelstan? Did she mistake desire for charm? After all, look at the way he watched Machara.

The music began and the thought disappeared as the steps brought them together. She was further intrigued because Adelstan could dance. Quite well, in fact, his steps fluid and graceful. They pressed their hands flat against each other, palm to palm, and a ripple of awareness rushed through her entire body.

How could she react so strongly to such a simple, innocent contact? She felt alive when she touched him, and she wanted—nay, yearned—to know more about him.

He smiled down at her, his green eyes sparkling, and she laughed gaily, happy he had come into her life. At least when she left Scotland, she would be leaving with him, someone she could build a friendship with.

But ye don't want to be his friend. Ye want to be his lover.

Her pulse quickened when he took both her hands in his and they moved to the right, then to the left, their bodies touching, his arm brushing her breast, making the blood in her veins sing.

His scent enveloped her, a purely masculine smell that made her weak at the knees.

"You must be excited knowing you will be lady of your own fief very soon."

"I would be happier knowing ye were staying on at Castle Almeron."

He looked confused by her answer. "Why is that?"

"Because I like ye, Adelstan." She smiled, seeing myriad emotions play over his face.

FOUR

"Ye were right. He *is* incredibly handsome. Not even handsome, but positively beautiful."

Rhiannon put her finger to her lips, but Elspeth merely laughed under her breath. "Aye, and he has lovely broad shoulders and a high, tight arse. I can see why ye are smitten with him."

"I am not smitten with him."

Elspeth smiled coyly. "And yet we are following him? Ye are smitten, Rhiannon, even if ye will not admit it."

Since meeting Adelstan last evening, Rhiannon could think of nothing but the tall, striking English soldier. She had kept Elspeth up half the night talking her ear off about him, relaying every bit of their conversation, and bragging about what a graceful dancer he had been.

After a few hours of sleep, Rhiannon had awoken, dressed, and kept a vigil by her chamber window, waiting for any sign of the handsome English knight to appear.

When she had finally caught sight of him exiting the tower and heading down the long staircase to the bailey below, her heart had jolted and she had rushed into action.

With cowls over their heads to hide their identities, she and Elspeth followed Adelstan to the stables, where he spent less than five minutes, and exited with horse in tow. He waved to the guard overhead in the gatehouse and stopped to talk for several minutes, before continuing on his way.

Rhiannon, dragging a complaining and tired Elspeth with her, walked into the stables, intent on catching up with Adelstan.

Antony, looking sleepy and disagreeable, immediately brightened upon seeing Elspeth, and it helped the maid's spirits, too, apparently, for soon the two were locked in a heated embrace.

Rhiannon took Nessa, her stepmother's favorite horse, out of spite, knowing the woman doted on the animal more than anything or anyone.

Not particularly fond of horse riding since witnessing a servant being trampled to death as a child, Rhiannon preferred instead to walk, much to her father's censure. Now she wished she'd taken a more active interest.

With reins in hand, she walked out of the stables. "Elspeth, we must go."

The maid gave Antony a final kiss.

"Are ye sure about this?" Elspeth asked, taking her by the hand. "What if he discovers us following him?"

"We will say we are out for a ride."

"At this time of morning? He will never believe it."

"I do not care, Elspeth. I want to do this. If ye do not want to go with me, then I understand."

Elspeth glanced past Rhiannon's shoulder to the road ahead, before meeting her gaze once more. "I shall go."

Rhiannon hugged her. "Thank ye."

They crossed the bridge out of the castle, and could see Adelstan at a distance, riding at a slow gait.

They mounted the horse, a task that took longer than it should have. Elspeth was as unskilled with horses as Rhiannon, but somehow they managed. Her father always insisted a lady ride sidesaddle, and that was exactly why she rode astride now. At least in this position she had balance and felt more in control.

They rode for miles, and Rhiannon began to get anxious when Adelstan cut off toward the path that led to a pond surrounded by trees.

Tethering his horse, he walked to the pond's bank, then reached behind his head and lifted his tunic off.

"Oh, my goodness, he's lovely. Just lovely," Elspeth whispered, an appreciative smile spreading over her face.

Rhiannon held her breath as Adelstan placed the tunic over a tree branch. She wondered if he took such care because of the extensive, delicate embroidery at the neck and sleeves. Someone had taken great pains to sew the design. She ignored the stab of jealousy at the thought of who that woman might be.

"Oh my," Elspeth breathed with a wicked grin. "What a lovely body."

Indeed, Adelstan's chest was wide and pleasing to the eye. His stomach toned, the definition of his abdominal muscles bunching with the slightest movement.

Her own abdomen tightened, along with her nipples.

Removing his boots, he then tugged at the cord of his braies, pushing them down past his lean hips, before stepping out of them. Just like with his tunic, he placed the braies over the tree branch.

Rhiannon held her breath for a moment.

He was turned so she could not see his cock, but she could see the high, firm globes of his buttocks.

"Will ye look at that arse," Elspeth said absently, biting her lower lip. "I swear the man is without a single flaw."

Rhiannon could only nod in agreement, her throat too tight to speak. Now this was what a man should be. Broad shouldered, a narrow waist, long, strong legs.

Then he turned and both Rhiannon and Elspeth released a gasp.

"God's breath, the man is truly blessed," Elspeth said, adding a moan for good measure, her hand moving to her heart. "Bloody hell, he is as thick as my wrist."

Rhiannon did not have to ask what her maid meant by such a statement. In fact, the fingers of her right hand encircled her left wrist. "Aye," she agreed, not daring to blink as a burning need filled her.

Adelstan's cock was not just thick but long, and it made her feel all tingly inside, especially between her legs, as she continued to stare at his impressive appendage.

"He is more man than most women could handle," Elspeth murmured, and to Rhiannon's horror, Adelstan turned and looked in their direction, his green eyes narrowing as he scanned the brush.

Elspeth's fingers wrapped around Rhiannon's upper arm and they both froze. She would die from humiliation if he discovered them.

Thankfully a flock of geese flew overhead.

Watching their flight, Adelstan walked into the water and then disappeared beneath the surface.

"We must go before he sees us," Rhiannon said, her eyes glued to the water, her legs made of stone. She couldn't leave if she wanted to. They had come too far to flee so soon. Plus, what would it hurt to watch just a little while longer?

"Soon," Elspeth replied, barely blinking, her full attention on the pond.

"What if we are caught?"

"No one will come, and we are well hidden."

Adelstan broke the surface and swam the length of the pond, his strong, muscular arms stroking the water with practiced precision.

Elspeth glanced up and Rhiannon followed her gaze. The skies were dark, and in some places pitch black. And they were a good distance from the castle.

To make matters worse, lightning flashed just as Adelstan broke the surface. He glanced up at the sky while treading water, looking not at all concerned.

The rain started slow but with each minute the drops grew larger, and pounded down on the once still pond. Even Adelstan noticed it would not let up, for he started swimming back toward the shore.

Elspeth shifted a little. "It's raining so hard. I wonder how long it will last."

"I think we should go."

She nodded.

With a lingering look at the pond, Rhiannon followed Elspeth out from their hiding place and toward the area where they had left their horse tethered.

But Nessa was no longer there.

"Where the hell did she go?" Elspeth asked, looking wildly about. "This is exactly where we left her, I'm sure of it."

"Shh," Rhiannon said, lifting a finger to her lips. "Aye, this is the right place. She must be around here somewhere."

God's breath, this could not be happening!

Chances were good Adelstan would be out of the pond by now and soon would be dressed. Any minute now he could come upon them and realize what they were doing there.

"Ye must not have tethered her tight enough."

"But I did!" Elspeth exclaimed, clamping her hand over her mouth.

Rhiannon's breath caught in her throat. Hopefully with the rain falling and the distance between them, Adelstan would not have heard Elspeth's raised voice. Taking her by the hand, she rushed away from the pond, hoping to catch the horse.

When they had run a short distance, Rhiannon dropped her hand.

"Do ye know how long it will take us to walk back to the castle in this rain?" Elspeth said, clearly agitated. "Your father will be furious with both of us, but most likely he'll have my head."

"I'm sorry, Elspeth. This is all my fault. I could not help myself."

The maid nodded in understanding. "Do not worry, lass. Nessa cannot be very far, and we'll be back at the castle before anyone realizes we are gone."

Lightning flashed in the sky and thunder roared. Elspeth shrieked yet again.

"Elspeth," Rhiannon whispered under her breath.

Elspeth winced. "Sorry."

Frustrated with herself more than Elspeth, who had come only out of duty to her, Rhiannon picked up her pace, damning the horse that had abandoned them. Given her luck, she would be struck by lightning.

Mayhap that would not be so horrible, after all. At least then she would not have to marry an old Norman knight, and spend her days pining away for a man who could never be hers.

"Perhaps Nessa will return to the castle, and Antony will come searching for us," Elspeth said, hope in her voice as she caught up to Rhiannon.

"Perhaps," Rhiannon replied, hugging herself. "We should not have come."

Elspeth did not say anything, though Rhiannon knew she most certainly would agree. Now if Rhiannon could only forget what she had seen at the pond. Adelstan's amazing body and his impressive cock.

Though she shivered, her insides burned with an inner fire that no amount of rain could cool. In fact, now that she had seen all of him, she wanted him even more desperately.

Worse still, she realized she would not rest until she knew Adelstan Cawdor intimately. Aye, never had she desired another as much as she desired the English knight. "I cannot believe we did this," she said more to herself than to Elspeth.

"I can," Elspeth said with a saucy smile. "The man is sinfully beautiful."

Rhiannon glanced over at her friend. "Aye, he is, isn't he?"

"Aye, in fact, I think he is the most handsome man I have ever seen. No wonder all the women in the hall watched him last night. Had I been there, I probably would have, too. His body is as beautiful as his face, and he is large where it counts most." Elspeth sighed. "Nothing like a nice big cock to make a woman sigh with pleasure. Of course, being that big, it would be hard to take it fully."

"Scandalous woman," Rhiannon breathed, ignoring the throbbing of her sex at the maid's description of Adelstan's manhood.

Elspeth laughed coyly. "What I could do to that man."

"Stop it," Rhiannon said, pushing away from Elspeth, who frowned at her.

"Ye truly fancy him, don't ye?"

"I do not," Rhiannon said, a touch too quickly.

"Rhiannon, ye would not have followed him all this way had ye not liked him just a little."

"I should be struck by lightning."

Elspeth frowned. "Why, because ye desire a man? That is pure nonsense."

"He is not my intended, though."

Elspeth shrugged. "It does no harm to look."

"Aye, but looking only makes me want him more."

"Ye are not married yet."

"So that makes it right?"

"It does not make it wrong. We cannot help who we are attracted to, just as we cannot help who we are *not* attracted to. I cannot imagine the thoughts going through your head, my dear. To learn your betrothed is older than your father has to be disconcerting."

"Aye, it is."

They walked in silence and the rain let up a little, but not for long. More black, angry clouds rolled in overhead.

The quiet gave Rhiannon time to think of her future and her actions. Her father would be more than furious to hear she had been spying on Adelstan.

44

True, Adelstan was handsome—to be sure—but what did she really know of the man? He could be mean and cruel for all she knew.

Plus, she was to marry another man, and her future set in stone. Once she married, she could never have sex with another.

Ever.

Before her death, her mother had cupped Rhiannon's face and said with a soft, sad smile, "Rhiannon, I hope one day ye shall know true love."

Back then she could not guess at her mother's sorrow. How horrible to love a man who did not love you in return, and watch as he fell in love with someone else. How helpless she must have felt.

Did her mother ever have a secret longing for another man? she wondered.

"Lady Rhiannon, is that you?"

"Bloody hell," Elspeth muttered under her breath.

Rhiannon turned slowly to find Adelstan sitting astride his horse, holding Nessa's reins in one hand.

"Adelstan, what on earth are ye doing here?" she asked, hoping she at least sounded surprised.

She glanced at Elspeth, who stared at Adelstan with mouth open. Apparently she could expect little help from her dumb-struck friend.

Adelstan's surprised expression gave way to a smile that made her heart skip a beat.

"Look, Elspeth, I believe Adelstan has found our wayward horse," Rhiannon managed to say, now thankful for the cool rain that splattered against her suddenly heated cheeks. "We were out for a ride, and the horse it, um, leapt up—"

Elspeth's fingers bit into Rhiannon's upper arm.

Dear lord, she was blathering like an idiot.

"She was probably frightened by the thunder," he said, dismounting.

Rhiannon shifted on her feet, hoping Elspeth would speak up and say something.

Anything.

Elspeth blinked a few times, an odd smile frozen on her lips.

Adelstan's hair was soaked from the recent swim and the rain that continued to fall. The blond locks stuck to the side of his neck, droplets disappearing into the vee of his tunic, where the slightest bit of olive skin showed.

Aye, she remembered every inch of that lovely flesh. Her nipples extended against the kirtle and she guessed he noticed them by the direction of his gaze.

"I had gone for a swim, and when I returned to my horse, I found another grazing beside him." His gaze shifted over her once more, stopping for a moment at her waist, and lower still. Indeed, he could probably make out even more of her person through the soaked garment of her light-colored kirtle.

His gaze slowly wandered to Elspeth, before returning to her. "So you said you were thrown from the horse?"

"No," she blurted at the exact same time Elspeth said, "Yes."

Please God, strike me dead.

Rhiannon could feel her cheeks grow hotter by the second, especially when Adelstan's brows knitted in confusion.

"Not thrown as much as fell," Rhiannon said, hoping he accepted her explanation. Her knees were a bit dirty from where she'd been kneeling in the brush spying on him, so the lie didn't seem altogether impossible.

Elspeth nodded. "Aye, that's exactly the way it happened. Just what she said. It is fortunate ye came along, or we would be in a bad way, to be sure. Aye, we would be in a—"

"He understands," Rhiannon said, a tight smile on her lips.

Adelstan turned his attention to Elspeth. "I do not believe we met last night. I am Adelstan of Braemere."

"I am Lady Rhiannon's nur—"

"Maid," Rhiannon interjected, the sound of *nurse* seeming far too young.

"I am Elspeth. A pleasure it is to meet ye, Adelstan of Braemere."

"It is nice to meet you as well, Elspeth." Adelstan brushed a hand through his wet hair. "I had forgotten how fast the weather can change in Scotland. I am surprised the two of you journeyed so far from the castle." He looked up at the angry sky. "Your father must be worried sick."

"Well, he doesn't exactly know we left."

Adelstan's lips curved in a smile that had her heart skipping a beat. "He said you were stubborn and strong-willed, and I have to say he might be right."

"Did he?" Rhiannon asked, not at all surprised her father would say such a thing to a virtual stranger.

While he looked elsewhere, Elspeth stared boldly, her gaze sliding down his body slowly and stopping at, of all places, the large bulge between his thighs.

Rhiannon coughed, and Elspeth's gaze ripped back to his face.

Adelstan looked at her with concern. "See, you have probably caught cold already. We had best return to the castle. Would one of you ladies like to ride with me?"

FIVE

Would she like to ride with him?

Excitement rushed through Rhiannon and she nearly tripped over herself to say yes when Elspeth started walking straight toward Adelstan's horse.

Disappointment ate at Rhiannon's insides as she followed behind, forlorn that she was stuck riding Nessa. That is, until Elspeth sidestepped Adelstan and tried with little success to mount Deirdre's miserable excuse for a horse.

God bless her! Adelstan walked over to Elspeth and told her to put a hand on his shoulder. He helped her mount before returning to assist Rhiannon, and settling behind her.

Rhiannon yearned to lean back against him, to feel the hard expanse of his powerful chest and rock-hard stomach pressed against her back. Instead she held her back rigid, but was fully aware of the heat coming from him.

"It is a long way to the castle. You may as well rest against me," he said, his breath warm against her neck. And he smelled lovely, a fresh scent mingled with his own original essence. A scent she would never forget.

"I do not wish for ye to be uncomfortable." How breathy her voice sounded!

"I am not uncomfortable, Rhiannon."

Rhiannon. Not Lady Rhiannon, just Rhiannon. She smiled despite her effort not to.

Slowly she leaned against him, and had to swallow a sigh. His body felt wonderful, so warm and strong. They fit perfectly together, as though they were made for each other. Savoring his heat, she nuzzled closer.

To her shock, she felt something suspicious against her bottom and lower back.

"You must be freezing," he said, his arms resting lightly against her thighs.

"Aye, a little," she said, her teeth chattering.

"I think more than a little," he said, humor in his voice, his large hands on either side of her upper arms. The next second he was moving them up and down her arms in an effort to warm her. Goose bumps rose on her flesh, not from cold, but rather from excitement. She closed her eyes, well aware Elspeth could be watching the exchange. She just hoped Adelstan did not feel the sudden acceleration of her heart.

"Does that help?"

"Aye," she said, her voice low and husky.

"Tell me the truth. Where were you headed when you were thrown from the horse?"

Her heart leapt. Had he seen the two of them spying on him? "Out for a ride."

"On a day such as this?" He sounded surprised.

"We live in the Highlands, Adelstan. 'Tis unusual if it does not rain," Elspeth said with a wink that made Adelstan laugh, and Rhiannon grinned, pleased with the maid's quick thinking. "We are accustomed to such weather. Plus, we do not like sitting indoors and sewing all day. We are of tough Scottish stock, after all."

"I've no doubt of that, Elspeth, but even tough Scottish women should know better than to leave the castle and not bring a cloak with them."

"But ye didn't either, Adelstan."

"Aye, but I am used to the cold."

Rhiannon heard the humor in his voice and smiled. She glanced back at him, her heart hammering in her breast. How handsome he was with his hair wet, and slicked back from his beautiful face. "When we left the castle, it was not raining."

"Nor did we plan to journey so far," Elspeth added, which was the truth.

"I am surprised your father allows you such freedom given the fact these are times of war."

"My father has little say in what I do." She tried to keep the edge from her voice but failed.

He stared at her, his gaze slipping to her lips. Her stomach tightened. Was that desire she saw in those light green depths, or was she seeing only what she wanted to see?

He licked his bottom lip and Rhiannon did the same. "Do ye have any other siblings, aside from your brother?"

"Bac is my half brother, born to Deirdre while my mother was still alive. She made no effort to hide the pregnancy, and when he was born, my father jumped at the chance to call him his legal heir."

"I am sorry, Rhiannon." He reached up, touched her cheek

with the back of his fingers. "It is my hope that you will find happiness in England. I know how difficult it is to leave one's home, but in this case, perhaps a new beginning is what you need."

"A new beginning with a man old enough to be my father?"

He looked away for a moment, and Rhiannon could tell he was choosing his words carefully. "More often than not in these cases, the man is older than the woman."

"Lord Malgor is older than my father, Adelstan."

He nodded. "I know."

She turned forward and rested against him. "The rain is letting up, I think."

"I do not mind the rain. In fact, the weather in northern England is not so different than in Scotland, though we get a little less rain than you do. I have been to Castle Almeron and there is a lot that will remind you of the Highlands, I think."

"Such as?"

"There are lots of trees surrounding the castle itself, as I mentioned before, and a river. England has its fair share of lakes, rivers, and ponds. You shall not be without a place to swim."

Her eyes narrowed. "How do ye know I like to swim?"

"Because last evening when you arrived in the hall, the ends of your hair were wet. That, and your stepmother said you enjoyed swimming."

"Aye, he is right. I love the water."

"As do I," he said absently, then quickly added, "so do not fret. Your new home shall have water aplenty in which to swim."

"What of Braemere?"

His eyes lit up at the mention of his home. "Braemere also sits above a river but the water moves very fast so one must be careful."

"Braemere sounds lovely."

"It is."

"When will we be leaving?"

He seemed surprised by her question. "As soon as you are ready. My liege understands you might need time to say your good-byes."

Was he anxious to return home? she wondered. No doubt he had a life to get back to and mayhap a woman, too. The selfish part of her wanted to keep him here, to get to know him better, but to what end?

He would never be hers.

He would deliver her to de Cion, witness the marriage, and then leave for Braemere, and she would never see him again.

The sooner they left, the shorter time they had together, to get to know each other, and the sooner her life would begin with Lord Malgor.

If Adelstan's liege said he would give Rhiannon as much time as she needed to say her good-byes, then she would take as much time as possible.

The heat of his entire body enveloped her, and she closed her eyes against the warring emotions inside her. What would it be like to have him as a lover? To have those arms around her, embracing her, comforting her always, touching her as he made love to her every night.

She remembered the day before when she'd watched Elspeth and Antony make love, and for a moment she envisioned herself and Adelstan making love on the forest floor, among the tall trees and wild flowers. The blood in her veins heated, coursing through her body, making the flesh between her thighs tingle and grow damp.

"Lord Malgor loves horses. He will be most pleased to learn you do as well."

Rhiannon opened her eyes. "Does he?" she asked, hating the way he kept turning the conversation back to her betrothed and to her future home. "To be honest, I prefer to walk most places. I only take a horse when absolutely necessary."

He laughed under his breath and she looked back at him. "Ye think me silly because I do not like riding?"

"Not at all. My mother never cared for horses either."

"I am glad to know I am not the only one, though I must say, Elspeth does not like horses either."

She stared at his hands and strong forearms.

"My hands are cold," she said, placing her hands flat over his, the palms covering the tops of his long fingers. She felt him shift in the saddle and she looked back at him. His light eyes slipped to her lips again.

She was entering dangerous territory and well she knew it. She could remove her hands, look away, sit up straight, and behave like the lady she had been raised to be.

Or she could lift her chin just so and kiss him as she was desperate to do. Elspeth would never breathe a word of it to anyone, nor would she judge her.

Plus, Rhiannon wanted desperately to feel what those lips would taste like. Just once. That's all she needed, she told herself. One kiss and she could walk away, content to have tasted him.

She glanced to where Elspeth had ridden ahead.

It was now or never.

Her insides twisted in indecision. What if he denied her? Would he tell her father of her scandalous behavior or, even worse, tell his liege or de Cion himself?

Taking a deep breath, Rhiannon turned in the saddle and looked up into Adelstan's incredible eyes.

His brows furrowed. "Rhiannon, I do not—"

Before he could utter another word, she touched her lips to his, softly, tentatively.

Her heart soared to the heavens when she felt the slightest pressure of his lips against hers. As small as that response was, it was still a response.

She held on to the horse's mane with one hand, while the other pressed flush against his chest. Boldly, her tongue stroked the seam of his lips and he made a purely masculine sound, a deep-throated moan that mingled with her sigh. His mouth opened and his tongue traced the recesses of her mouth.

Never could she have understood the intimacy of a kiss, and how truly beautiful it felt to share such an act with someone she cared for.

And she did care for this English knight who had been a stranger to her the day before.

One of his strong hands moved up her side, making the hair on her arms stand on end. Her heart pounded nearly out of her chest and she could feel his racing against her palm.

The sky opened up, rain falling down on them in large drops, but she didn't care. In fact, it only added to the intensity of the moment.

Adelstan's fingers tightened around her arms, and he abruptly pulled away, breathing hard, looking at her with a startled expression.

She could see the realization of what they had done on his handsome face. His throat convulsed as he swallowed hard, his gaze shifting to her lips before shaking his head as though to clear it.

"We cannot do this, Rhiannon. I have a duty to my liege to bring you back to Almeron so you can marry Lord Malgor. You must never speak to anyone about this, not even your maid, is that understood?"

Her heart plummeted to her feet. For a second she had experienced paradise and she didn't want it to end.

Rhiannon lifted her lips to his again, but he shook his head. Even his eyes had changed. "Nay, we cannot."

Her pride bruised, Rhiannon faced forward, her hands returning to her lap, her back ramrod straight.

"You can lean against me, Rhiannon."

"Nay," she said firmly, not caring if she sounded like a child.

"Rhiannon."

"I—I made a mistake, and I hope ye do not think less of me for it."

Adelstan's mind and body had never been in such conflict. He had gone to the pond to bathe and to rid his mind of the images of Rhiannon as they had danced last night. Everything from her smile to her sweet laughter had replayed in his mind since meeting her, making sleep nearly impossible.

Never had he imagined to be in such a quandary. His orders had been clear—bring Lord Malgor's betrothed to him at Almeron, safe and sound. That was it, plain and simple, then he would return to his life at Braemere.

And what did he do but kiss the very woman he had sworn to protect.

Fool.

Why had he not just accepted the hot bath the servant had so generously offered upon waking? Adelstan had declined, knowing a morning swim would not only ease his warring emotions but cool his heated body. And the swim had indeed done him good. He had left the pond resolved to do his duty by his liege, and to look at Rhiannon MacKay as he would any other married woman.

And yet when he came upon Rhiannon and her maid on the road back to the castle, he'd wondered why fate would put her in his path at the very moment he had pledged not to touch her.

A difficult thing when she stood before him soaked to the skin, her yellow gown clinging to her charms. It had been impossible to look away from her full, high breasts and the rose-colored nipples that had pebbled from the cold, poking against the fabric.

And he had felt those nipples pressed against his chest when she kissed him. Even now his lips tingled from that kiss, and for the life of him, he couldn't put two words together. The sky crackled again, and he tightened his hold around her, resisting the urge to rest his hands on her thighs.

Such young, firm thighs. He envisioned those same thighs, spread wide to receive him.

He closed his eyes and counted to ten, trying hard not to think of her naked. He had seen the look in her eyes, knew she would not deny him.

She is another man's betrothed.

"I did not mean to offend ye, Adelstan."

She looked over her shoulder at him, and those rare eyes of hers showed anger, mixed with vulnerability.

"You did not offend me, Rhiannon. Not at all."

As she looked into his eyes, he could not help but wonder how de Cion would react upon seeing her for the first time. He would be the envy of men everywhere. No doubt the newly titled baron would be delighted he had gained such a beautiful woman as his bride. His mistress, on the other hand, would hate Rhiannon on sight.

In fact, Adelstan did not trust the woman.

He could not get involved. Rhiannon's fate was sealed, as was his. One day he would meet the woman he would marry, and this day would be nothing but a memory.

"Did ye not like my kiss?"

His heart constricted. She was so beautiful, her dark lashes spiked from the rain, making her incredible eyes even more astounding.

"I liked your kiss, Rhiannon. Very much."

"Then why do ye reject me?"

"You know the answer."

"But I am not married yet."

"But you will be. I have made a pledge to my liege to protect you from harm, and I shall do just that . . . even if it means protecting you from myself."

Her eyes narrowed. "That is ridiculous."

"Perhaps, but I gave my lordship my word."

"What of your heart?"

"You are to be married, Rhiannon."

"I am not married yet, Adelstan."

He sighed heavily. Her father had been right calling her strong-willed and outspoken. "Aye, but soon you shall be living at Castle Almeron with your husband."

"I wish ye were my betrothed."

"Do not say such a thing."

"Why? I do wish ye were my betrothed. If ye were, I would willingly take my vows. In truth, I would rush to do so in order to make love to ye."

Her words heated his already boiling blood. His cock jerked against his braies. "Rhiannon, you must be careful what you say. If someone else were to hear, you could be charged with treason."

"No one is about, Adelstan. No one but the two of us and Elspeth, and she would never say anything that would harm me. Plus, I am not married yet, and there is no harm in an unmarried woman telling an unmarried man how she feels."

Castle MacKay sat in the distance, and Elspeth hung back now, waiting for them in the trees.

As they approached, the castle guard yelled out, and by the time they had crossed the drawbridge, Laird MacKay was walking in long strides toward them. His gaze shifted from Rhiannon to Elspeth. "Rhiannon, do not ever leave here again without my permission, is that understood?"

Adelstan remembered her saying her father never cared where she went, and he wondered if the concern he showed now was for his benefit, to make him look the loving father, when he wanted nothing more than to be rid of her.

"Aye, Father," she said with little emotion, slipping from the horse before Adelstan or anyone else could assist her.

"It is my fault," Elspeth said, quick to defend her mistress. "I was saddened by news of my ailing grandmother, and I needed to escape the castle to clear my mind."

Laird MacKay stared at his daughter and her servant. "Ye put your mistress in danger, Elspeth. Mayhap I need to reconsider sending ye to England with her?"

The blonde paled under the laird's cold stare.

"Father, Elspeth did not ask me along. I knew how sad she was, and I hoped to ease her pain by going with her. It was not a wise decision and I regret it. Please do not punish her for my foolishness."

Adelstan's nails bit into his palms. He had no right to interfere, but he also could not sit by and watch Rhiannon lose the only person she cared about, for something so foolish as taking a ride during a storm.

Rhiannon looked close to tears as she embraced Elspeth.

"Do not let it happen again, Daughter."

Rhiannon nodded, looking physically relieved, as did the maid. "Aye, Father."

Laird MacKay glanced at Adelstan. "How did ye come to be with them?"

"I went to the pond for a morning swim, and upon my return I found them huddled beneath a giant oak, taking shelter from the storm. They would have stayed longer, but both were concerned about you, knowing you would be sick with worry."

There was no way of knowing the laird's true thoughts, but all that mattered was he nodded. "Well, it is good ye came upon them when ye did, and now it is time ye have a warm bath, change into dry clothing, and take refuge from this blasted storm."

The laird looked at his shivering daughter with little expression, and Adelstan recalled last night when he had beamed upon seeing his son.

Having been loved by both his parents, Adelstan felt a wave of compassion toward the young Scottish beauty who, without waiting for her father's acquiescence, walked arm in arm with Elspeth toward the bailey.

As Adelstan watched Rhiannon disappear inside, he tried to get the image of her bathing from his mind.

Lord help him, but the days ahead would be the hardest of his life.

SIX

Rhiannon sat back in the bath, staring at the fire blazing in the grate. Elspeth sat by the chamber's only window and hummed an old Celtic tune while mending a tunic. "I think ye must care for Antony more than ye admit, else why would ye work so tirelessly on repairing that old tunic for him?"

Elspeth looked up at Rhiannon, her brows furrowed. "How do ye know it's Antony's tunic? Mayhap it is my grandfather's."

"I have seen your grandfather, Elspeth. He is not that small."

Shrugging, the maid continued humming.

"Do ye love Antony?"

"Nay, but I care for him. I enjoy being with him."

How fortunate Elspeth was to pick her own lover without thought of consequence. If only Rhiannon could do the same.

Elspeth set the tunic aside and stood. "Ye are melancholy, Rhiannon, and have been since our return. What happened between ye and Adelstan after I rode ahead of ye this morning?"

Rhiannon dropped her gaze to the steam rising off the water. "Nothing."

"Ye have never been able to lie to me, so do not start now." Elspeth walked behind Rhiannon, and began soaping her hair.

Rhiannon closed her eyes, remembering the touch of Adelstan's lips against hers, and that split second when she had forgot both time and place. He had kissed her, and he had liked it, the small moan telling her that much.

"What happened? Are ye angry that I left the two of ye alone?"

"Nay, I wanted ye to leave us alone."

"That is what I thought," Elspeth said, a smile in her voice. "Else I would not have done so. Tell me what happened."

"I think I made a mistake."

"A mistake. In what way?"

"I kissed him."

She heard Elspeth's quick intake of breath, but she recovered quickly. "And did ye enjoy the kiss?"

"Aye, very much."

Elspeth's laughter floated to the high ceiling. "Then why so grim?"

"After we kissed, Adelstan told me we should not have done so. He reminded me yet again that I am betrothed to another, and in essence we can never be." Rhiannon leaned her head back and looked up at Elspeth. "I shall never have him. I saw the look in his eyes, and could tell he felt deeply that he had betrayed his liege, who entrusted him to bring me back to de Cion untouched. How odd he should feel so horribly, while I, on the other hand, feel no guilt whatsoever."

"Perhaps ye are reading too much into his reaction."

"I saw the truth in his eyes, and the eyes don't lie. I'm afraid he will not betray his liege, no matter how much his heart and body tell him differently." Rhiannon shrugged. "Perhaps he feels nothing for me and was only saving me the agony of telling me so. At this very moment he could be laughing at me and thinking I am a fool."

"Ye underestimate the power ye have over him, my dear."

Rhiannon's heart missed a beat. "What do ye mean?"

Elspeth moved to the side of the tub. "I saw the look in Adelstan's eyes when he stared at ye this afternoon. He desires ye, I have no doubt of that."

"But ye did not see the way he stared at Machara last night during supper. He wanted her, and I know she wanted him, too. Every time she walked by, Adelstan had this strange look about him. He desires her."

"Do ye honestly believe a man would desire Machara over you?" Elspeth looked amused. "Trust me in this, ye are far more beautiful than ye will ever know. That is part of your beauty, ye have absolutely no idea how every man stumbles over himself whenever ye as much as look his way."

Rhiannon laughed under her breath, knowing Elspeth exaggerated in order to make her feel better. "Every man but the one I want."

"Every man has a breaking point. Ye just have to find out what Adelstan's is."

"I think I know it already. He will not break his pledge to his liege."

Elspeth's fingers curled around the tub's edge. "Once ye leave here and arrive at Almeron, all your chances will be lost. If ye like him, then let him know it. If he does not respond, then flirt with another man to see if it gains his attention. If ye do this and he reacts, then ye know he cares more than he will ever admit. Just be careful and do not let your father see ye do this, or Deirdre for that matter."

"What if Adelstan doesn't respond? Perhaps he told me the truth. Perhaps he truly regretted kissing me."

Before she could argue further, Elspeth lifted a pitcher of water and poured it over Rhiannon's head.

Running her hands down her face, Rhiannon wiped the water from her eyes. "Ye could have given me fair warning."

"Ye need to listen to me, love. Quit sulking and stand up, brush yourself off, so to speak, and go on as though ye never kissed him. Make him wonder where your thoughts are, and if he brings up the kiss again, tell him ye were caught up in the moment, scared of leaving Scotland and everything ye know and love."

"He will not believe me."

"Of course he will. If ye say it as though ye mean it."

Elspeth set a drying cloth on a rack before the fire, and shrugged into a cloak. "Now quit worrying about what is done. Tomorrow is another day, and all will be well."

"Where are ye going?"

Elspeth smiled softly. "Antony asked to meet me in the stables."

"The stables? How romantic," Rhiannon said, trying to keep the sarcasm from her voice.

"Believe it or not, there are few private places within the walls of Castle MacKay."

"Have a lovely time," Rhiannon said before Elspeth slipped out the door.

She eased down into the water, wondering where Adelstan was

right this minute. Closing her eyes, she envisioned him as he'd been earlier today. He was so strong, so handsome, so appealing to her in every way. Indeed, she could not think of a single fault or one thing she would change about him.

Even now her body burned for him. She touched her lips, remembering the feel of his mouth against hers, the stroke of his tongue, the velvety soft texture.

Looking over her shoulder, to be sure she was indeed alone, Rhiannon's hand slipped beneath the water's surface, resting on her breast, imagining it was Adelstan's hand.

Fingers splayed, she cupped the mound, weighing it in her hand before plucking at the rigid peak of a nipple. Gasping at the wonderful sensations that rushed through her body, Rhiannon touched herself in her most intimate place with her other hand and ran a finger over a hard little nub of flesh that had her shifting her hips.

Elspeth had been right. Touching herself could be pleasurable.

Leaning her head back against the tub's edge and closing her eyes, she continued to explore, envisioning Adelstan's strong, yet gentle, long-fingered hands touching her.

Her heart rate increased by the second as her fingers played over her tiny button and nipple. She arched her hips as a wonderful sensation lifted her higher and higher.

Tendrils of heat pooled in her groin, and then it happened; her sex throbbed against her fingers, and she moaned low in her throat as she experienced her first orgasm. She bit her bottom lip to keep from crying out.

Long moments later she opened her eyes and stared up at the

ceiling, trying to catch her breath. Her hands fell away from her body and she washed them, as though that would wash away what she had just done.

She felt a sudden rush of embarrassment, but it soon fled as realization dawned on her. Soon she would be married and her husband would touch her just like that. He could do what he wanted, when he wanted, and there was nothing she could do or say to stop him.

Rhiannon had once heard that if a married woman took a man other than her husband to her bed, then her husband would have cause to kill her.

And yet, even knowing that threat, Rhiannon still wanted Adelstan.

Adelstan paced the great hall. His men had finished eating long ago. A few played cards or chess, or conversed while servants scattered about, picking up empty trenchers, bowls, and tankards.

Machara, the comely servant who had served him last evening, caught his eye from across the room. She had been watching him under lowered lids all evening, and though he found her attractive, he could not get Rhiannon or the kiss they had shared this morning from his thoughts.

It did not help that he waited expectantly for her to appear in the great hall. God's breath, but he felt like a boy of eight, waiting for his first crush to appear.

When Rhiannon had not arrived for supper, he had been disappointed and wondered if it was his rejection that had kept her from the hall. Elspeth, her maid, had appeared late during the meal, but after speaking to a handsome young man at a lower table, she had sauntered off before he could have a word with her.

Adelstan had been compelled to follow her out, to ask of her mistress's health, but he could not without risking suspicion. After all, he had been sitting beside Laird MacKay, who had not mentioned his daughter once all night.

Jorden came up from behind him and clapped him on the back. "In case you have not taken note of the obvious, a certain servant has been lingering in yonder doorway waiting for you to take notice of her."

Adelstan smiled. "I have noticed."

"I thought so," Jorden replied, bringing a tankard to his lips. "My question is why do you remain here when you can be experiencing the sins of the flesh?"

He glanced in Machara's direction to find her watching him, a coy smile on her lips.

"Most of the men have already retired for the night. Go, take what the wench has to offer." Jorden pushed him in Machara's direction.

Adelstan ignored the warring emotions raging within him. His body ached for release.

Machara smiled widely at his approach.

"Where shall we go?" he asked, ignoring the hoots from his men as he reached for the woman's hand and led her from the hall.

"Wherever ye wish."

"You know the castle better than I."

Machara licked her lips and Adelstan could not help but compare them to Rhiannon's fuller, plumper lips. The lips of an innocent. His stomach clenched, wondering if he had been her first kiss. A strange mixture of emotion rushed through him at the thought. First kiss. First touch. First lover.

He was walking a dangerous line.

The inner bailey was still alive with activity, mostly officers and servants mingling.

"We will not be bothered here," Machara said, opening a door. The smell of bread rose up to meet him.

Adelstan pushed the door closed and pulled Machara into his arms. They kissed feverishly and he could not help comparing the experienced, rough, almost desperate kiss to the innocent one he shared with Rhiannon hours before.

"I have wanted ye from the moment I first saw ye."

"As did I," he whispered against her lips, cupping a full breast, tugging at an erect nipple. Though he had not had sex for a week, his cock was only semihard.

He took one of her hands in his, and brought it down to his erection.

Her eyes widened and she licked her lips. A moment later she fell to her knees, and with trembling hands pulled the cord of his braies.

His hands rested on her shoulders as she took him into her hot mouth. Oh yes, he needed this, a woman's soft mouth on his cock, sucking him, her tongue stroking the length of him from base to tip.

As she continued to suck his length, he let his head fall back on his shoulders and closed his eyes, envisioning another woman, this one with violet eyes and light brown hair with faint blonde streaks. He remembered Rhiannon's sweet body outlined in her soaked kirtle.

His cock lengthened more.

Machara cupped his balls and he put her at arm's length, his cock slipping from her mouth. She looked up at him, a knowing smile on her wet lips.

"Ye are so large," she whispered before his cockhead disappeared in her mouth again.

He leaned back, resting against a large, wooden table. Machara's tongue swirled around the crown, while her fingers gripped the base, balls and all.

He fisted a handful of hair and she moaned in delight.

SEVEN

Rhiannon had skipped supper for two reasons. One, she had no desire to see Adelstan, even though she had been unable to keep from thinking of him all evening. And two, she had lost her appetite.

Elspeth had brought up a plate to her chamber but the smell did little to entice her, and she ended up setting it out in the hallway, certain one of the castle's dogs would find and devour it. Or mayhap a hungry tower guard.

After her bath, Rhiannon sat before the fire in nothing but her chemise, wondering what on earth she would say to Adelstan when she saw him again.

Mayhap she could say she'd taken ill and was feverish.

Rhiannon looked down at the book in her hand. She had read the same page six times and could not calm her mind enough to take the words in.

Setting the book aside, she paced the chamber and looked at

the large canopy bed with distaste. Sleep was the last thing on her mind. Perhaps she should go in search of Elspeth, who was probably still with Antony in the stables. The fresh air itself would do her good.

Browsing through Elspeth's wardrobe, Rhiannon ended up choosing a rough, russet-colored cloak and a pair of well-worn slippers, both of which should not draw attention to her as her own finer clothing would.

Shutting the chamber door behind her, she rushed down the stairs swiftly, pulling the hood up and over her hair.

Her father would have a fit if he found her out wandering this time of night by herself, and in nothing but a chemise and cloak. She could only hope he was sound asleep by now.

Exiting the tower, she took a sharp left to the middle ward, a place she often went to find solace. However, that had been in the light of day and at night the middle ward was pitch black, save for a few torches here and there. Picking up her pace, she came to the doorway that served as a hallway into the inner ward, and it just so happened to set between the chapel and bakehouse. She opened the door slowly, and closed it, releasing a sigh when no guard called out.

How tempted she was to go to the stables to find Elspeth, but she would not steal away what little time the maid had with her lover.

She peeked into the inner ward and saw a group of soldiers lingering nearby. Damn! What were they still doing up at this hour?

Waiting for a heart-pounding minute, Rhiannon looked out into the inner ward again and spotted one of Adelstan's men-at-arms. The handsome man with dark hair and piercing silver eyes laughed at something one of the others said, his teeth flashing white in a wolfish smile.

If she took a chance and walked right by Adelstan's friend, would he allow her to pass without giving her true identity away and alerting the others? She had a feeling he might keep her secret, but would her father's trusted soldiers?

A strange noise carried out into the night, coming from the vicinity of the bakehouse. Who on earth would be there at such a time? Had Elspeth and Antony met here instead?

Nervous, Rhiannon inched toward the door, which was already slightly ajar, but she could not see anything through the tiny space. Pushing the door open a little more, she looked inside and her heart gave a hard jolt upon seeing Adelstan. She nearly said his name, but was stopped short of doing so when she realized all was not right. She could not see all of him, but his head fell back on his shoulders, his eyes were closed, his mouth slightly open, and he breathed hard.

A feminine moan came again, and Rhiannon opened her mouth in outrage when she opened the door a sliver more to find Machara on her knees, sucking Adelstan's cock.

Though part of Rhiannon wanted desperately to slam the door, she knew doing so would make her look extremely childish and jealous.

Damn him!

Adelstan shifted on his feet, his fingers gripping the whore's hair, his hips slowly pumping against her mouth.

"Do ye like that?" Machara asked, one hand holding his hard cock still as she smiled up at Adelstan, who nodded, his eyes heavy-lidded.

"Ye can come whenever ye like. I do not mind. Ye can make it up to me another night."

Having brought herself to orgasm, Rhiannon knew Adelstan must be experiencing the same or similar sensations. If only that were her mouth on Adelstan's cock instead of the servant's, whose head now moved back and forth with great speed.

Adelstan's thick length, slick with saliva, disappeared and appeared in rapid succession. As she stared, Rhiannon's nipples grew sensitive, and heat wove its way through her veins, down low in her belly, to her sex, which pulsed with the need to be filled.

Machara's hands cupped the high cheeks of Adelstan's ass as her mouth worked him into a frenzy. A deep, primal moan vibrated from within his chest, and Rhiannon felt it all the way to her bones.

Adelstan thrust a few more times, and released a pleased moan as he reached climax, pumping slowly against the servant's mouth.

His hands cupped Machara's cheeks, and he smiled softly, obviously pleased with her performance. Machara went back on her heels and smiled up at him, wiping his seed from her lips with her fingers.

Rhiannon noted Adelstan's cock still appeared semihard. Her own sex tightened looking at him, envisioning the large length inside her now weeping sheath.

Her body burned for him.

"Tomorrow night I shall make it up to you," Adelstan said, pulling up his braies and tying them.

"I shall count the minutes until then," Machara said, a confident smile on her face.

Rhiannon rolled her eyes and ignored the piercing envy that nearly choked her.

Adelstan reached for Machara and kissed her gently. The woman sighed, her arms encircling his neck. Rhiannon took a step backward, being careful not to alert the two in any way.

However, Machara must have seen her from the corner of her eye because she gasped. A second later Adelstan whipped open the door.

"Lady Rhiannon," he said, looking alarmed.

Rhiannon pretended to be closing the chapel door behind her. She hoped he could not see how red her cheeks were. Indeed, it was all she could do to make eye contact with him.

"Good evening, Sir Adelstan," she said, hoping she sounded surprised. Rhiannon didn't look at Machara, but she noted the woman's hand rested possessively on Adelstan's bicep.

"Are you coming from the chapel?" Adelstan asked, shutting the bakehouse door behind him.

Rhiannon nodded. "Aye, I could not sleep, so I decided that perhaps prayer would help."

Machara's brows rose, but she remained quiet.

Rhiannon intentionally let her gaze shift from Adelstan to Machara and back again. "What are the two of ye up to?"

"Machara needed my assistance."

The servant's lips quirked.

"This time of night?" Rhiannon asked, not bothering to hide the sarcasm in her voice.

"Aye," Adelstan said quickly. "Machara, did you get everything you needed?"

Machara glanced up at Adelstan. "For tonight," she said, dropping her hand to her side. "I shall see ye on the morrow?"

"Aye," Adelstan replied, and waited until she walked off, leaving the two of them alone.

"Lady Rhiannon, let me walk you back to your chamber," he said, reaching for her arm, but she stepped away from him.

"That is not necessary," Rhiannon said, walking toward the gate she'd just passed through.

"Do ye often leave your chamber unattended?"

"Nay, only when Elspeth is occupied."

"Why do you go by way of the middle ward? It is dark, and you could run into trouble."

"The only person I fear is my father."

"Why is that?"

She turned to look at him, and almost wished she hadn't. He was so gorgeous. "Because he looks for me to do wrong in order to punish me." She had meant to say it lightheartedly, but it didn't come out that way.

"I find it hard to believe that is so."

Rhiannon shrugged. "Believe what ye will, Adelstan. It is not easy for me to come and go as I please like ye do. Ye may sulk around the bakehouse with a comely servant, but I, on the other hand, am not as fortunate."

He straightened a little, his green eyes narrowing. What had Elspeth said . . . to use her wits? She need not act like a jealous wife. After what she had just witnessed, she seethed with jealousy, but by damn, she would not show it. "Is that why you are dressed as you are? So you can come and go as you please?"

She had forgot about the borrowed cloak and slippers. "Aye, it is." She cleared her throat, uncomfortable with his direct gaze. "I am sure ye are tired after your sport, so I shall let ye go."

"Rhiannon, please."

Ignoring him, she pushed the door to the middle ward open

and slipped through. A rush of wind blew the hood back, along with the cloak, the chemise whipping about her legs.

Rhiannon made no move to cover herself, especially seeing where Adelstan stared. She wanted him to look.

"You must be cold," he said, grabbing for the edges of the cloak, trying to bring them together, but she pulled away.

Rhiannon's heart skipped a beat as he looked down at her, the nerve in his jaw twitching. Despite her resistance, he caught the edges of the cloak together and pulled the material tight about her. "You shall catch your death." He pulled the hood back over her hair. "Why did you leave your chamber dressed in so little?"

"I needed to think."

"About?"

"My future."

His gaze shifted over her face. "It is not wise to go out at night. A man might see you and get the wrong impression."

"What kind of impression? That I am a servant who is out searching for a lover?"

She could not believe she had been so bold to say those words, and yet she felt a certain vindication having done so, especially when she noted the strange look of guilt in his eyes. He wondered if she had seen him with Machara or not, and was no doubt at this moment curious as to just how much she had seen.

Let him wonder.

"Who goes there?" a loud, booming voice said from the ramparts.

"Do not say a word," Adelstan said, putting an arm around Rhiannon's shoulder and pulling her close. She reveled in the heat and strength of his body flush against her own.

"It is I, Adelstan of Braemere."

"Good evening, sir," the guard called, a knowing smile on his lips. "I suggest ye stay to the inner ward. It is well lit."

"Thank you," Adelstan replied as he turned and walked back through the gate. "Keep your head down and put your arm about my waist. No one should stop us, and if they do, I shall do my best to protect your identity."

Rhiannon slipped her arm around his waist and smiled inwardly when she heard his quick intake of breath.

They stepped into the inner bailey, and Rhiannon had to walk fast in order to keep up with Adelstan's long strides. Someone called out his name, and she felt him lift his free hand in greeting. He pulled her closer. "We shall be at the tower shortly."

With each step toward the tower, the more she savored the feel of his touch . . . until the memory of what she had seen moments before in the bakehouse flashed in her mind.

Her emotions were in turmoil. Part of her wanted to tell him exactly how she felt about him, and the other wanted to berate him for having been with Machara just hours after she had all but thrown herself at him. If he longed to be with a servant, then he had every right to be, and there was nothing she could do about it.

It might take time, but if she could keep Adelstan at Castle MacKay, then perhaps she could, little by little, win him over.

But to what end?

Nothing would change her future. She would marry Malgor de Cion, even if Adelstan did become her lover. And what then? Would they spend their lives always looking for a bakehouse or some other quiet building in which to make love?

"Good night, Rhiannon," Adelstan said, stopping at the base of the tower stairs.

"Ye come no farther?" she asked, her brow lifted in surprise.

"I would hate for your father to wake and find the two of us alone together."

She lifted a brow. "Ye are afraid of my father?"

His eyes narrowed. "Nay, I am not afraid of your father."

"Then walk me to my room." She ascended the steps, not waiting to see if he followed. Feeling his gaze on her back, she smiled inwardly.

Stopping at her chamber, she turned back to look at him while opening the door. "Would ye like to come in for a moment?"

He swallowed hard, and shook his head. "I cannot."

The cloak slid from her, and she tossed it over a chair, aware his light eyes followed her every movement. "Come in for just a moment. I swear I shall not bite."

"Where is your maid?" he asked, taking a step in, but the door remained open.

"With her lover."

He flinched as though she had struck him.

"Does that surprise ye?"

"No, but hearing you say it does."

"Ah, ye think me unladylike."

His lips curved softly. "Nay, I do not think you unladylike, Rhiannon."

She straightened her shoulders, and pressed her hands to the small of her back, knowing full well the stance pushed her breasts out. "My back aches from this morning's ride."

She could tell he fought to keep his gaze at eye level. "Is that why you missed supper?"

"Aye," she said, despite the fact it was not the truth.

Liquid fire rushed through Adelstan, and it was all he could do not to pull Rhiannon into his arms and kiss the coy smile from her lips.

The moment he'd walked out of the bakehouse and found her standing there, he had been consumed by guilt.

But why?

She was hardly his woman, and yet he felt compelled to put her mind at ease, to let her know that Machara—or any other woman for that matter—could not hold a candle to her.

Her long hair licked at her high buttocks, the chemise hiding absolutely nothing from his gaze. Now she walked toward the fire, standing before it, her slender back taunting him as she held her hands out to the flames.

He trembled with his need for her, and here, after he had just had his cock sucked by another. But in his mind it had been Rhiannon who had pleasured him, her mouth, her tongue, her hair he had fisted in his hand, not Machara's.

Dear God, she had bewitched him, this woman who was to marry another man. This woman he had sworn to keep from harm.

"Tell me something of my betrothed," she said, turning to face him.

The breath left his lungs in a rush.

He could see the outline of her body clearly through the white linen. Rose-colored nipples topped firm, full breasts, the small nubs poking at the material. Her waist was tiny, her hips flaring slightly. He could clearly make out the hair between her thighs, and his cock jerked against his belly. Thank goodness his tunic covered the evidence.

She tilted her head and his gaze ripped back to her beautiful face.

The face of an angel.

An angel, who knew exactly what she was doing to him. *Did she do this to torment him?* he wondered.

Of course she did. This was the same woman who had kissed him earlier today. The woman sworn to one of his fellow officers—a man he had fought many a battle with.

"Baron de Cion is well liked amongst his men."

She pressed her full lips together as she stared at him. "Ye said he was once married. What did his wife look like?"

"I do not recall. It was many years ago."

"Was she also young?"

"Younger than he, but not a great age difference."

"What color was her hair?"

"I think it was dark."

"Like Machara's?"

The side of her mouth lifted in a smirk and he knew in that moment she had witnessed his tryst with the servant.

"Do ye like dark-haired women, Adelstan?"

"I like women."

She laughed a little, but he also sensed her frustration with him. "I'm a woman. Do ye like me?"

"I think you already know the answer to that, Rhiannon."

Warning bells were going off in his head, especially when she walked toward him, her hips swaying in time to the pounding of his heart.

She stopped just shy of him and looked up at him with those haunting violet eyes the color of Scottish heather. "Show me how much ye like me, Adelstan."

Conscious of the nearby open door, and the fact her father slept directly above her, Adelstan refrained from touching her. "My duty forbids me to act on my feelings."

"So ye do feel something for me, even if your duty keeps ye from doing anything about it?"

His throat was suddenly so dry that he could only nod.

She dragged her teeth along her lower lip, the action sensual without her meaning it to be.

Or perhaps she had meant it to be and was not as innocent as she claimed.

That would be the easiest explanation.

But what if she was an innocent and she truly did desire him? Never before had a woman gotten under his skin so quickly as Rhiannon. Was it the fact she was forbidden that made her so appealing to him?

"I can keep a secret, Adelstan. I can and I shall."

He could hear his heart pounding in his ears, the sound so loud he barely heard footsteps just outside the door. Before he could react, the door pushed open and Elspeth appeared.

The maid looked from Adelstan to Rhiannon, her mouth curving in a wide smile before she restrained it. "I did not mean to interrupt."

"I was just leaving," he said, brushing past Rhiannon. To his dismay, his upper arm grazed her breast. He ground his back teeth together, his need for this woman so intense, it unnerved him.

A hand enveloped his for a moment, and he turned to look down at her.

He almost wished he hadn't. Those violet eyes were so dark with unspent passion, he was half tempted to lock her maid out and take her right then and there.

"Thank ye for walking me to my chamber, Adelstan. Perhaps we shall run into each other in the bakehouse again?"

Was that an open invitation?

While his body throbbed at the promise of such a request, his mind told him to run as far and as fast as he could from Rhiannon MacKay.

EIGHT

"Ye saw Adelstan and Machara together in the bakehouse?" Elspeth asked, pulling a chair before the fire.

"Aye, and they were having sex."

"Oh, Rhiannon, I am sorry."

"I saw it all. The way he looked at her. The way his hands slid through her hair. I swear sometimes I wish I were a servant. At least then I could choose who I made love to." Easing the ache from her shoulders with her hands, Rhiannon tried without success to get the image of Adelstan and Machara from her mind.

"I might have the ability to pick my own lover and not worry I will be forced to marry, but otherwise, my life is not my own."

Rhiannon nodded. "I know that, Elspeth. I do, and I do not wish to sound ungrateful for all that I have, but I swear I would change places with ye right now if I could."

"Come, no more frowns, my dear. Tomorrow is another day."

"What if we ran away?"

"Rhiannon, ye cannot be serious?"

"Aye, but I am. Do ye think Antony would leave with us?"

Elspeth's brows furrowed. "I do not know. What of your marriage to Lord Malgor?"

"I am certain Lord Malgor can find another bride, and he earned Castle Almeron on his own."

Elspeth smoothed her hands over her skirts. "Once he learns how truly beautiful ye are from the soldiers who return, he will be furious to know ye slipped through his fingers."

"I could never be happy with him, Elspeth. I know it in my heart."

"When de Cion dies, ye shall claim everything he possesses, including lands and wealth."

Rhiannon could care less about lands, titles, and wealth at the moment.

Elspeth poured warm wine into a goblet. "Here, perhaps this shall help ease your mind."

"Numb my mind, ye mean."

Motioning for Rhiannon to sit on a bench before the fire, Elspeth began brushing out her hair.

Rhiannon took a long drink of the wine, her mind still racing with all she had witnessed this night. "Damn, but I cannot rid myself of the image of those two together." What had Adelstan said to Machara? *Tomorrow night I shall make it up to you.*

Not if she had anything to do about it.

"Ye must put Adelstan from your mind if ye are to have any peace."

If only she could.

"Tonight, when he walked me back to my chamber, I saw the way he looked at me. I admit I took off the cloak in order for him to see my body. I wanted to see if he desired me the same way he desired Machara."

"And did ye get your answer?"

"I don't know for sure. I thought I saw a heat in his eyes. Lord help me, but I want him desperately, Elspeth. I burn for him."

Elspeth hugged her from behind, and rested her head on her shoulder. "Ye will not rest until ye have him, will ye?"

Rhiannon set the goblet down and turned. "Nay, I will not."

Elspeth smiled. "That is what I thought."

"So what can I do?"

"Remain here as long as possible, then ye might just have time to win Adelstan over."

"But how do I win him over, especially now that he has found a lover, and one who is much more experienced than I?"

Elspeth's lips quirked. "Seduce him."

"I do not know how."

"Ye are already well on your way, but ye must be aggressive with a man like Adelstan, who puts duty and loyalty above all else." Elspeth's brows drew together. "First off, ye must understand what making love means. I could try to explain it to ye, but it would be best if I could show ye what I mean," she said absently. "Aye, ye must see for yourself. It is the only way ye will truly understand."

Realizing what Elspeth was suggesting, Rhiannon's heart rate increased. She was not about to tell her friend she had already spied on her and Antony making love.

Taking a deep breath, Elspeth looked at Rhiannon, her gaze intense. "I am meeting Antony again tomorrow night in the stables. Ye can watch us from up in the loft."

"Ye want me to hide in the loft?"

Elspeth nodded slowly. "I will not tell Antony ye are there, and ye must be very quiet. I mean it, Rhiannon. Ye cannot let out a single peep or be discovered, or he may never forgive me."

Surprised Elspeth would be so willing to help her in this matter, Rhiannon nodded. "I swear I will be as quiet as a mouse. Neither one of ye will know I am there."

"I doubt that," she said, running a hand down her face. "Ye can never say I don't do anything for ye."

"Thank ye, Elspeth. This means a lot to me."

Elspeth crossed her arms over her chest and paced the chamber. "Until then, ye must gain Adelstan's attention. Seduction is not all about making love. It's the way ye look at a man, talk to him, or just make him feel. Moments alone are scarce, so ye must create them. In fact, the men are riding out first thing in the morning to hunt. They will be gone all day, but when they return, ye must be where Adelstan can see ye."

"What if I fly the falcon?"

Elspeth lifted a brow. "Excellent idea. And we shall have Mortimer, the handsome young guard, come along."

"Do we need a guard?"

"Of course, if only to make Adelstan jealous. And your father will be pleased to know we did not venture out alone."

Rhiannon smiled, already excited for tomorrow to come. "Then that is exactly what we shall do."

Adelstan grinned inwardly as Jorden boasted of his ability with bow and arrow, the evidence of which had been flung over the back of a pack horse they had brought along for such purpose.

An impressive kill.

His soldiers were excellent hunters and each had proved his skill this day. Castle MacKay and its occupants would eat well this night . . . and for days to come.

"I hear ye spent the evening with the pretty servant," Jorden said, brushing sweat off his brow with the back of his hand.

The few men within earshot chuckled.

"Aye, I did, but only a little while."

"Long enough, aye?"

Adelstan nodded. "Long enough."

"There was a day you used to tell me everything."

"The difference being, we were boys back then."

Jorden winked. "We'll always be boys, sir."

"Speak for yourself," Barden replied, a smirk on his thick lips. "Between us, de Cion's bride makes me hard." He rubbed his cock. "A rare beauty that one, and her tits are like ripe m—"

"That is enough," Adelstan said, his voice coarser than intended.

The good-natured Barden looked alarmed, where Jorden merely looked amused.

"I meant no disrespect," Barden said.

"I know." Adelstan clapped him on the back reassuringly. "I know."

Barden walked off, and once he disappeared, Jorden turned and looked at Adelstan, arms crossed over his wide chest. "A bit touchy when it comes to the lass."

He couldn't even defend himself, not with Jorden. "I know."

All night he had been unable to shake Rhiannon from his thoughts, or forget her violet eyes as they stared into his, or the unasked question as she had looked from him to Machara. If he hadn't known better, he would say Machara had wanted Rhiannon to know what had happened.

Rhiannon had said she'd been leaving the chapel, but was that the truth? And if she had watched, just how much had she seen?

"She is attracted to you as well."

Adelstan frowned, and Jorden glanced away, his gaze focusing on Dante, a young knight who had recently joined de Wulf's ranks. The knight had signed on to travel north to Castle MacKay when he had found Jorden would be doing the same.

The two had been making eyes at each other all day. It reminded Adelstan of Lady Rhiannon last night, and the way she'd looked at him. But had he been seeing what he wanted to see or what was really there?

"Are you so used to sleeping in quarters with your men, that when you are awarded a private chamber, you find sleep long in coming?" Jorden pushed a hand through his dark shoulder-length hair, and cast a glance at Dante again. The newly knighted soldier was helping another knight tie a stag to his horse. "Or mayhap you missed my company?"

Adelstan laughed under his breath. "Nay, I never sleep well when I am away from Braemere."

"Nor do I, my friend," Jorden said, stretching. "A fine day. Shall I rally the men?"

Adelstan glanced up at the fair skies. "It is still early enough that we have time to stop by the loch in order to wash away the remains of the hunt. What say you?"

Jorden's eyes lit up. "Excellent idea, sir."

"I thought you might think so."

A quarter of an hour later, Adelstan swam out into the deep

dark water of the loch, wondering how he would handle matters with Machara this evening. After last night she would want, or rather expect, him to meet up with her and finish what they had started, and yet, he lacked the desire to do so.

Plus, he could not get Rhiannon out of his mind, or how she looked last night in nothing save her chemise.

Rhiannon is forbidden fruit, his mind said, and yet his body said something altogether different.

Which meant he would indeed meet Machara this evening, if only to remind himself that Rhiannon was not his, and would never be. Mayhap he would even invite the servant to his private chamber.

"Sir, we are heading back," Barden said, motioning toward a group of soldiers who were already dressed.

"We shall be along shortly," Adelstan replied, still feeling bad for having spoken so tersely to him earlier.

Adelstan swam out farther into the loch, enjoying the feel of the cool water against his heated loins. He loved swimming, enjoyed the release it brought, both body and mind.

He returned to where Jorden stood waist deep in the loch, busy scrubbing his hair. Dante lingered nearby, his wide blue eyes sliding slowly over the older knight's powerful body. Only one other soldier remained, too busy dressing to take notice of the flirtation going on in the water.

Adelstan grabbed a handful of sand from the loch floor and scrubbed his scalp. He enjoyed the nature of Scotland, the crisp air, the scent of firs and heather. The beauty of its women.

He caught Jorden's gaze and knew his friend wanted him to leave. With a nod, Adelstan did just that, and was surprised when seconds later Dante followed him out of the water.

Drying himself off with his tunic, Adelstan dressed quickly and walked toward his horse, who grazed nearby. Dante lingered on the bank while Jorden stepped from the water, letting the air dry his body, and letting the boy look his fill, which he did.

Adelstan covered laughter with a cough as he mounted his horse.

"I shall see you both back at the castle in time for dinner."

Dante's face was flaming red. "Aye, sir!"

Jorden smiled wolfishly while pulling on his braies. "We'll be there, sir."

Feeling slightly guilty for leaving the boy behind, Adelstan headed out, riding his horse at a leisurely pace toward Castle MacKay. He knew his men grew uneasy being in Scotland for too long. The Scots were not exactly fond of King William and were therefore untrustworthy. However, before leaving Braemere, Renaud had told Adelstan to be sure Rhiannon was given ample time to say her good-byes to her father.

Despite her uncertain relationship with her father and step-mother, Rhiannon did have a connection to the land and its people. Everyone brightened upon seeing her, and she had a way of putting each at ease. Her leaving would be a huge loss to the people of Castle MacKay.

And in turn, she would become an asset to Castle Almeron, where her beauty would be sung about by minstrels and poets alike.

And once again jealousy and rage gripped at his heart, knowing another would claim her. She would make love to another man and give birth to that man's child.

He tightened the reins within his fist, the leather eating into his gloveless hands. He wondered what his liege would say if he rode to Braemere and told him he had made a mistake, and that he wanted Rhiannon for himself.

Already he knew what Renaud's answer would be. The deed was as good as done. Money had been exchanged, contracts signed. The only thing needed now was the bride herself, and the marriage would take place. And then the consummation . . . and then all was lost.

There was only one thing he could do.

Forget her.

NINE

In the meadow just east of Castle MacKay, two women and a tall broad-shouldered guard stood while a falcon flew high above them. Adelstan's heart leapt at the familiar figure wearing men's clothing.

Dark leggings clung to Rhiannon's slender legs and her tunic barely brushed the tops of her thighs. A large belt nearly swallowed her tiny waist, and chausses laced all the way to the knee.

His sister had dressed in a similar fashion from the moment Braemere had been taken from them and their parents killed. However, she had done so out of necessity and to keep focus from her. He had never thought anything of it, and yet now, he could see exactly why Aleysia's husband, Renaud, had been entranced by the sight. Something about a beautiful woman in men's clothing was intensely erotic, particularly *this* woman. Her long hair had been bound in a single plait that fell down her slender back, as thick as his wrist and bound with black ribbon.

What he would do with that ribbon if given the chance.

It seemed a few of his men had noticed Rhiannon and her attire, for she had an audience.

He caught up with them just as Rhiannon lifted her arm and the falcon landed on her gloved hand. Many of the men cheered, and she turned and gave a mock bow.

To his surprise, Dante and Jorden rode up, the latter looking a tad disappointed. Apparently the boy was playing hard to get.

"A shame de Cion is not here to see his betrothed," one of his men said with a knowing grin.

Barden remained closemouthed.

"He wouldn't make it to the wedding night if he were," another said.

Adelstan cleared his throat. "Return to the castle and prepare for supper." The men broke off, heading toward the castle, though their gazes kept straying to Rhiannon.

The side of Jorden's mouth rose a fraction. "I think it a good look for Lady Rhiannon, do you not agree, sir?"

"I had not thought about it."

He laughed under his breath. "Of course you hadn't. Will you be returning to the keep, or would you like me to see to your horse?"

"Why do I feel your kindness serves another purpose?"

Jorden narrowed his eyes, shrugged. "You know me too well, sir. Mayhap I feel the sudden urge to linger in the stalls with the knights."

Adelstan shook his head and dismounted, handing the reins over to Jorden, who nudged his horse's flanks and started toward the castle, Adelstan's horse in tow.

Walking in long strides toward the trio, Adelstan noted how

close the guard stood to Rhiannon. The man said something in her ear that made her laugh.

Jealousy coiled within Adelstan. As he approached, Rhiannon's servant looked at him with a welcoming smile. The guard noticed his approach, but other than a glance, he returned his full attention to Rhiannon.

Adelstan had at least a decade on the younger man, who had dark brown hair and warm brown eyes. He had never seen him before and wondered at the nature of their relationship.

"Adelstan, have ye come to watch Rhiannon fly her falcon?" Elspeth asked, sounding excited.

"Aye, I have."

The guard stepped behind Rhiannon, helping with the weight of the bird. "Now just like so," he said, his front flush against Rhiannon's back.

Adelstan's fingers itched to wrap around the guard's neck.

The falcon took flight and Rhiannon looked back at the guard, a wide smile on her face, which faded the second she saw Adelstan.

"Ye have returned from your hunt?" she asked, but looked away as she watched the falcon soar. "Look at her, Adelstan. Isn't she beautiful?"

"Aye," he said, not even glancing at the falcon, but rather staring at Rhiannon's profile. She had never looked so beautiful, her cheeks pink from the exertion, her eyes twinkling with awe, her lips split into a smile that made his heart pound.

"See the height she's getting?" the guard said, looking pleased. "It is as I said, Rhiannon. Speak softly to her and she will respond to ye. Just like any woman."

Adelstan fisted his hands at his sides, wanting the man to

leave, not at all liking the tone he used when speaking to her, or the fact he used her first name, without her title, when addressing her.

"Is he correct, Adelstan?" Rhiannon asked, lifting a brow. "If you speak softly to a falcon, will she do as ye ask, just like any woman?"

He watched her intently and saw the innocence in her eyes. But still he wondered of the barb.

Clearing his throat, he replied, "Aye, he is correct."

"I must return to the castle to help prepare for dinner," Elspeth said with a sigh. "Mortimer, will ye escort me back? I seem to have twisted my ankle."

The guard looked extremely disappointed to be leaving Rhiannon and even opened his mouth, but snapped it shut a moment later. "Of course. I shall be delighted to assist ye." He turned to Rhiannon. "Anytime ye need my assistance, Lady Rhiannon, I am at your disposal."

"Thank ye, Mortimer," Rhiannon said, smiling prettily. "I should like that very much."

As the two walked off, Adelstan took a step closer and watched as Rhiannon in turn kept her eye on the falcon's flight. "I do not have a lot of experience yet, but I hope what I lack in experience, I make up for with enthusiasm."

There it was again, that tone and certain innuendo.

She shifted on her feet, and it was all he could do not to drop his gaze past her lovely, full lips. Truth be told, he liked her spirited ways and frank manner of speaking.

A tendril of hair had escaped her plait and rested against a fragile collarbone. How he ached to reach out, touch that lock, wrap it about his finger. And yet he could not do so for fear of someone seeing.

She pursed her lips and let out a call. She had a mouth made for kissing. A mouth he *had* kissed, but only too fleetingly. How he yearned to do more. So much more. Teach her everything there was to know about making love. To touch every inch of her body, kiss every inch of her skin. Fill her sheath and give up every ounce of his seed.

The falcon started to descend and she held her arm up. "Can ye help me, Adelstan? She is a bit too heavy for me to handle on my own."

So that was how the other officer had come to be so close to her? Perhaps it had been innocent?

He nodded and stepped forward, standing behind her, just as the guard had done. She took a little step back until her buttocks brushed against his cock. He bit his bottom lip. Hard.

"Here she comes," she said, looking back at him, her violet eyes dancing. "Take my hand, Adelstan."

She said his name in a breathy way that had his heart skipping a beat, and his cock standing at attention.

Doing as she asked, he braced her arm with his own, his hands sliding beneath her gloved one. She pressed into him even more, and he could feel her heart pumping fast.

Was it because of the falcon, or from the contact of their bodies?

A second later the falcon landed on her hand, the beautiful bird taking the treat Rhiannon gave her. "You're so lovely," she breathed, her accent sending a shiver up his spine. She could have been talking to a lover instead of the bird, who reacted to her voice.

"Go ahead, Adelstan, talk to her. Say something sweet."

Sweat beaded his brow. He was not one for flowery words or poetry. Though educated from a young age, he had always preferred the manly pursuits of hunting, fighting, and war to romantic pursuits. Swallowing against a throat gone suddenly dry, he said, "You are a pretty bird."

Rhiannon's lips split into a smile. "Despite the fact I am younger than ye, I do believe there are a few things I could teach ye." There was that innuendo again.

God help him, but she was beautiful. She had to feel the hard ridge of his cock against her back, but perhaps in her innocence, she did not realize what she was doing to him. "And there are a few things I could show you, too," he said before he could stop himself.

The smile vanished and her gaze dropped to his lips.

He shifted, wishing he had not stopped, but gone directly to the castle. "What is the falcon's name?"

"Beatrice."

He could not help the laughter that came, and she scowled, though it didn't reach her eyes. "Ye do not like the name?"

"I did not say that," he said, trying to keep a straight face but failing.

She laughed, too, a soft, pleasant sound that made his heart pound even harder. "My mother's first bird was called Beatrice, and she loved it so, that I told her when the day came I could fly my own, I would call her Beatrice in memory."

"I am sure she would be most honored to know you have done so."

The laughter stilled on her lips. "Aye, she would."

"I like your attire."

She lifted a tawny brow. "Do ye really?"

He nodded. "Very much."

"Adelstan . . ."

"Yes?"

She pressed her full lips together, her gaze searching his. "I wish it were ye."

He frowned. "What do you mean?"

She released the bird a second later and, with her free hand, captured his hand, holding it between them so that no one could see, her fingers squeezing tight around his. "I wish it were ye I was marrying. I wish it were ye who would take me to my bridal chamber. I wish it were ye who would take my maidenhead."

Adelstan's heart roared in his ears. The air around them seemed to crackle. God help him, he wanted this woman in a way that terrified him. All his life he had lived by the sword and put his duty and honor above all else.

Until now. He felt his control, which he'd always called on, slipping as he looked into violet eyes that pleaded with him. He had to remember that he had been asked among all of Renaud's men to personally escort Rhiannon to Castle Almeron for her marriage to de Cion, his peer and fellow soldier.

God, strike me dead at this moment for my wicked thoughts.

"Ye are not saying anything, Adelstan."

Her throat convulsed as she swallowed hard. "Do ye not feel the same?"

The soldier in him yearned to scan the meadow and the castle walls to be sure no one watched or guessed at the nature of the conversation taking place. Yet the man in him refrained.

The woman he desired above all others was telling him she wished he would take her maidenhead, that she wished he would be her husband. And yet he stood silent, saying nothing.

She released his hand, took a small step back, and dropped her gaze between them.

"Rhiannon, look at me."

She shook her head.

"I would lift your chin with my fingers if I could, for I want you looking at me when I tell you this."

She took a deep breath, then looked up, and it was then he saw a shimmer of tears in her eyes.

It was nearly his undoing.

He took the small step that separated them. "Rhiannon, I desire you more than you will ever know, and yet, this cannot be. I was sent here on a mission, and I will do my duty to my liege. I will bring you safely to Almeron and to de Cion . . . with your maidenhead intact."

She brushed away a tear with the back of her hand before looking at him again. What he saw in her eyes now concerned him more than the tears moments before.

Firm resolve.

"I understand your duty, and while I commend ye for your loyalty to your liege, will ye ignore your heart?"

"Aye."

Her mouth opened and she crossed her arms beneath her breasts, pushing them up, nearly to her chin.

His mouth went dry.

"Ye are so stubborn, Adelstan. Ye would deny yourself what ye want when it's right in front of you, and for what—for the sake of honor and duty? Will honor and duty keep ye warm at night?"

He said nothing until he saw the falcon returning. "Beatrice," he said.

Rhiannon turned so quickly, she lost her footing and stumbled.

102

Steadying her, he regained his position behind her, his hand sliding beneath her slender arm, cupping her hand.

She leaned back even more, so that no space at all separated them. Indeed, the heat from her body made him sweat.

"Rhiannon," he said in warning.

He could not see her face, but he could imagine the smile there, the violet eyes that had been shimmering with tears seconds before now twinkling with glee. Her buttocks brushed against his cock, again and again, until he was gritting his teeth.

Would the fucking bird land already?

"Come to the meadow with me, Adelstan," she said, seconds before the falcon landed on her delicate, gloved hand. "Come to me. I beg of ye."

"I cannot, Rhiannon."

"Why?"

"How would we explain our absence?"

"If not today, then what of tomorrow? Elspeth and I can set out and ye can be our escort."

"This is a dangerous game, Rhiannon."

She stepped away, turned to face him. "It is not a game to me." Though the falcon had to be heavy, she did not struggle with its weight at all. She lifted her chin slightly, reminding him she was a nobleman's daughter, used to getting her way, no doubt.

"But it is a game, whether you want to admit it or not. We cannot do this, Rhiannon. It would be the biggest mistake of our lives. You do not understand what is at risk."

"I would risk *everything*," she said without blinking.

If only the blood didn't burn in his veins, or the ache in his groin would just cease. "You do not understand, nor will you ever."

She stared at him for a long moment, then frowned. "Ye do not desire me, do ye?"

She took a step from him, and he should have let her go, but he reached out, grabbed her wrist. "One day maybe you'll understand."

As though he'd said too much, he released her hand. She sent the falcon flying and took a step closer, pressed a hand to his cheek. "I do not want ye to leave me, Adelstan. Ever. I could not bear leaving my people, moving to a new country, and having you leave me at Almeron, before or after the wedding."

More than anything, he wished to tell her he would never leave her, but he could never make that pledge. He knew only one certainty—that she would marry Lord Malgor within weeks, if not days, of her arrival at Almeron.

"This is madness, Rhiannon."

"Nay, it is not."

"It is. It's an impossible situation and one we must remedy now. We can be friends, but only friends."

"I must forever be your friend and nothing more?"

"Aye."

"Or at least until de Cion is dead?"

He closed his eyes for a moment. "Do not say that."

"Why? I wish he were dead. I hate him with everything that I am."

He opened his eyes. She did not jest. She meant what she said. "How can it be that you wish the man dead and yet you have never met him?"

"Because he is keeping me from what I want most, and that is ye."

Adelstan ran a trembling hand through his hair. "We must return to the castle before someone sees us."

Her grip only tightened. He could see the curve of her breasts from his vantage point and yearned to touch them, to take a nipple into his mouth, suck and lave it.

"I see desire in your eyes when ye look at me. Lie to yourself all ye want, Adelstan, but one day, the inevitable will happen. We *will* be together. The need will consume ye, just as it consumes me."

God help him, but her words sent a shiver of awareness shooting through him.

She went up on her toes, whispered in his ear, "When I touch myself at night while I'm alone in my chamber, it is your hands I feel on my body."

Her declaration shocked him, and effectively spiked his need to a fever pitch. He'd had a hard enough time sleeping since meeting her, and now, it would be damn near impossible.

She dropped his hand and started walking toward the castle. Rhiannon whistled loudly, and the falcon followed overhead.

With a steadying breath, Adelstan walked behind her, watching the long strides, the way the tunic barely covered her heart-shaped buttocks.

When I touch myself . . . it is your hands I feel on my body.

That statement alone made him want to touch himself. Or perhaps he would find Machara again and finish what they had started. Perhaps then he would finally get Rhiannon MacKay out of his blood once and for all.

TEN

Antony could never be considered lazy, for the loft had been stacked full of hay. In fact, Rhiannon had to push a few large bushels aside in order to make a good hiding space for herself.

Thankfully, the gaps in the loft floor were just wide enough to see the stable below.

As she awaited Antony and Elspeth's arrival, her thoughts turned to the exchange between herself and Adelstan this afternoon. Had she succeeded in drawing him in with her flirtatious manner? She had been more than blunt. At first she had been disappointed when he told her they could never be, but then when he'd told her he desired her, too, she'd been excited. She had her work cut out for her, just as Elspeth had said, but she didn't care. She wanted Adelstan and she would stop at nothing to get him.

Honor and duty would always come first to Adelstan, but perhaps if he allowed himself the opportunity, he could love her.

The stable door opened, and Elspeth and Antony entered.

With heart racing, Rhiannon shifted the slightest bit in order to get comfortable, and something moved near her foot.

A mouse?

She bit her lip to keep from crying out, and shook her foot, hoping to scare the pest away. It seemed to do the trick.

Antony pushed Elspeth gently against a stable door, his hands cupping her face as he ground his lower body into her.

"Ye lusty boy," she said with a giggle, and Rhiannon saw her gaze shift once more to the loft.

"Ye think me a boy, do ye?"

"Nay, not that part of ye at least," she said, her hand moving between them, where she cupped his manhood. He responded with a throaty laugh before moving from her, just long enough to drop the latch over the door.

"No one should bother us for a while," he said, bending to kiss her. Elspeth's arms wrapped around his shoulders, and Antony's hands settled at her waist, while he rocked his hips against her.

They kissed for long, heated minutes, their mouths mating with a fevered intensity that reminded Rhiannon of their previous mating by the loch.

Perhaps it was the continual time restraints that caused the rush and intensity?

Elspeth dropped to her knees and fumbled with the tie on Antony's braies. She bit into her lip, looking quite determined.

"Ye're trembling, lass," Antony said, his hands resting on her shoulders, reminding Rhiannon of Adelstan when Machara had been sucking his long, thick cock.

Antony's braies fell to his knees and Elspeth glanced up at her lover with a knowing smile before taking his length into her mouth.

Rhiannon's heart picked up speed. Aye, this was exactly what had happened between Adelstan and Machara. The only difference being that Adelstan's head had been resting back on his shoulders, whereas Antony stared down at Elspeth, his fingers curling around her slim shoulders as he murmured heated words. Adelstan's hand had also been fisting the whore's dark hair.

Trying to forget about Adelstan for the moment, Rhiannon focused on Elspeth's movements, how she held her head, how wide her mouth was. With one hand Elspeth held the base of his cock, while another hand splayed against his stomach.

She laved the cockhead, her tongue swirling around the ridge before taking him all the way inside her mouth. Rhiannon wondered how she could do so without choking. Adelstan was much larger than Antony, so perhaps it was easier for Elspeth because of the size difference?

"I will come if ye don't stop, Elspeth."

Hearing the warning, Elspeth stopped and looked up at Antony with a coy smile. With his cock jutting out from his body, he helped her to her feet and turned her around. He lifted her skirts, but she swatted his hand away and shook her head as she walked toward the back of the stable to the stall beneath the loft where Rhiannon hid.

With a wicked smile Antony kicked his shoes and braies off, and reached behind his head to rip off the tunic and drape it over a stall door.

Elspeth removed her clothing, taking great care to hang the kirtle over the stall that had been cleaned and had fresh hay and a candle burning in the corner. "Looks like ye were expectin' someone."

He reached for her, pulled her into his arms. "Only ye, lass. Only ye." His fingers slid through her hair as he cradled her face and looked into her eyes. "Ye make me crazy with need, woman. I'm so hard for ye."

"We will get to that, but perhaps ye could pleasure me as I have pleasured ye?" Elspeth lay on the bed of hay, her legs parted slightly, her brow lifted as she waited for him.

A second later he was covering her, and kissing a trail from her lips, down her throat, to her breasts.

As she watched, Rhiannon's nipples hardened and grew sensitive against the linen of her chemise and gown. She cupped the firm mound, felt the bud stab her palm, and wished more than anything that it was she and Adelstan down in that stall making love.

Antony moved lower, down Elspeth's belly.

Stomach tightening, Rhiannon chewed her bottom lip. He wasn't going to . . .

Oh yes, he was.

Rhiannon's pulse skittered as Antony pushed Elspeth's thighs farther apart, before parting her nether lips—and kissing her slit, focusing his attention on the tiny button there.

Elspeth's mouth opened, and she closed her eyes, her fingers weaving through Antony's hair. Her hips arched against his face as he licked her, his tongue flicking in all directions.

Rhiannon could see her friend's reaction to what Antony was doing, and by her heated moans, she apparently liked it—nay—she loved it.

A cry escaped Elspeth's mouth and her eyes opened as she looked straight up at the loft. Although she had no way of knowing for sure, Rhiannon had a feeling Elspeth didn't see anything or feel anything besides white-hot pleasure.

Antony kept on, squeezing Elspeth's buttocks with his hands, licking her slit before lifting her clit with his long tongue.

Elspeth groaned loudly, which in turn extracted a deep, mutual moan from Antony that made Rhiannon smile. The maid's chest rose and fell heavily as she fought for breath, and she reached for her lover, pulling at his arms. With a wicked laugh, he climbed up her body.

Elspeth's hands moved up and down his back, her nails scraping a path from his shoulders to his waist and even lower, to his buttocks.

Antony reached between them, and though Rhiannon could not see what he was doing exactly, she assumed he was guiding his cock into Elspeth's body.

He began to move his lower body.

Rhiannon's heart raced and her stomach coiled as a strange fluttering began deep in her groin, between her thighs, making her women's flesh hot and wet.

The hay beside her foot moved again, and she felt fur brush up against her ankle. She kicked at it, and a shriek came from the critter.

Certain the two below had heard, Rhiannon chanced a glance down and saw they had not paid any attention. Indeed, they were in a different world.

A world I want to experience.

Hoping her furry friend would go to the other side of the loft once and for all, Rhiannon wondered where Adelstan was at that very moment.

The candle fluttered when Antony flipped so that Elspeth was now on top, astride him, her hands resting on his chest, her long blonde hair brushing his thighs and belly as she rode him.

As Elspeth began to move, Rhiannon couldn't help being reminded of how she felt whenever riding a horse astride.

Antony sat up a little and kissed Elspeth's breasts. Elspeth rode him harder and faster, the sound of skin slapping against skin vibrating throughout the stables.

The horses seemed not to take notice of the lovers, aside from the annoying Nessa, who watched with interest.

Elspeth moved faster and faster before crying out with pleasure. Antony's hands slid to her waist, holding her steady as he lifted his hips against her, groaning as he found his release.

Rhiannon eased onto her back and folded her hands beneath her head, letting the lovers have a quiet moment to themselves. She was thankful and grateful to Elspeth for letting her watch such a private experience.

Adelstan stood up on the ramparts, looking out to the southeast, wondering what was happening at Castle Braemere, his family's fief in the north of England.

If only he had his twin to talk to now, he would ask Aleysia what to do and how he should handle the strong-willed Rhiannon MacKay.

No doubt Aleysia would smile, perhaps laugh, and tell him to follow his heart . . . just as he had told her to do thirteen years ago when Renaud de Wulf had stormed into Braemere Castle and made a bargain that had sealed both their fates.

Thirteen years.

Had it really been that long?

He had watched his sister and brother-in-law throughout the years. Their happiness and obvious love for each other had always warmed him, and yet now that same devotion also reminded him of what he was missing and might never have.

No woman had ever come along to make him consider settling into a fief and spending the rest of his life defending his castle and lands while raising a family.

Until now.

Rhiannon MacKay tempted him to throw away everything he had worked so hard for, for so many years.

What did he really know about her, besides the fact she had lost her mother, whom she obviously had loved and adored. Also, her relationship with her stepmother and father was volatile, and with her half brother, nonexistent.

He had seen it happen before in families, especially when an older man took a younger wife. The old wife and children were oftentimes tossed aside, forgotten.

Adelstan felt, rather than heard, someone behind him and turned to find Jorden stepping from the shadows. "I hope I didn't startle you," he said with a warm smile. "You seemed a million miles away."

The concern in Jorden's face warmed Adelstan. "I was."

"You missed both dinner and supper. The men wondered if you had taken ill after the hunt."

Down in the bailey a guard set torch to lamps placed every ten yards. "No, I am well. Just weary."

Jorden rested against the rampart wall, his silver eyes assessing. "You are too young to have your body ache after a hunt. Perhaps you need to increase our drills."

His soldiers were the finest in England, pushed to impeccable condition in order to protect Braemere at all costs. "Perhaps I shall."

"Or mayhap your weariness stems from another matter altogether."

Adelstan lifted a brow. "I'm surprised you're not in the company of a certain knight."

His white teeth flashed in the night. "You wish to change the subject. Very well, I had every intention of finding Dante, and I did. He was near the stables, where he happens to linger each night, waiting for the stable master. Apparently the two enjoy a friendly game of chess. The odd thing is, tonight the stables were locked."

"Locked?"

"Aye, bolted from the inside." Jorden pushed away from the wall, walked to Adelstan, and leaned over the battlements. "Dante said he saw Lady Rhiannon enter just after supper."

Adelstan frowned. "You think it is Lady Rhiannon who is locked in the stables?"

"Dante said Rhiannon's maid and the stable master entered not long after she did." He lowered his voice. "The three have been locked in ever since."

Adelstan's stomach twisted. "I do not believe it."

Jorden flinched as though struck.

"I did not mean to imply—"

"I understand, my friend."

When I touch myself . . . it is your hands I feel on my body.

Since meeting the Scottish lass, Adelstan had wondered about her frank speech, bold looks, and the way she spoke freely about touching herself. Perhaps she knew much more about making love than what she let on.

I wish it were ye I was marrying. I wish it were ye who would take me to my bridal chamber. I wish it were ye who would take my maidenhead.

"Perhaps I shall check on her myself," Adelstan replied, his gaze shifting to the stable doors and the sliver of light beneath.

"I shall have your back, sir."

Adelstan nearly told Jorden not to follow behind just in case he found Rhiannon in a compromising position, but knew his friend would not take kindly to being told no. "Swear to me that no matter what we find, you will not speak of it to anyone."

Looking hurt that Adelstan would question his loyalty, Jorden nodded. "Of course. You have my word."

The two made the bailey just as the stable doors opened and a couple appeared. Adelstan's heart skipped a beat when he recognized Elspeth and the stable master. Relief washed over him in waves. Jorden must have been mistaken. Rhiannon must have left beforehand. Perhaps she had gone looking for Elspeth and had exited as quickly as she'd entered.

"Mayhap I was wrong," Jorden said, watching the two share a passionate kiss. "The maid is quite comely, is she not?"

"Aye, she is," Adelstan agreed, the relief he felt making him grin like a boy. "Her name is Elspeth."

Elspeth put her lover at arm's length and plucked straw from his hair. She cradled the stable master's face with gentle hands and kissed him again.

"Come, let us leave them alone." Adelstan walked toward the keep when Jorden reached out a hand and grabbed him by the wrist. He pointed to a dark hallway that opened on the far end of the stables.

At first Adelstan didn't see what Jorden pointed at, until a slight figure emerged from the hallway, dressed in the same familiar old cloak she had worn just last night.

Rhiannon.

His blood ran cold.

She had told him she never went out by herself at night, and yet here she had done so two nights in a row. And last night she'd worn only her shift beneath the cloak. Had that been for her lover's benefit?

Adelstan pulled Jorden back into the shadows. "Do not tell a soul what you have seen."

"I already gave you my word, sir."

Adelstan turned and looked into his friend's silver eyes. "I trust you."

Jorden's mouth curved. "I trust you, too." A dark brow lifted. "Look, there she goes."

Rhiannon looked left then right and, seeing the path clear, slipped out into the inner bailey, making her way quickly toward the tower.

Adelstan's fury grew by the second.

He knew full well what the three had been up to, and yet a part of him couldn't accept that she was far from innocent. Jorden himself had told him the stable door had been locked from within. There was only one explanation for that, and even more damning was the fact that Rhiannon had left by way of a different exit so anyone seeing wouldn't assume the three had been together.

Is that why she had shown so much interest in Adelstan? Had she wanted him to make love to her so she had someone else to blame for her lack of maidenhead come the morning after her nuptials?

Dear God, what if she were already with child?

Devious woman.

Elspeth pulled her cloak over her blonde curls, and nearly ran right into them.

"Elspeth," Adelstan said, and the woman gasped.

"Good evening, sir." She glanced at Jorden, smiled.

Jorden nodded, his gaze shifting over Elspeth slowly, making the stable master uncomfortable. The man slid a possessive arm around her shoulders.

"How are you this evening?" Adelstan asked, nodding in greeting to the man at her side. The stable master was handsome, though his nose was a bit too large for his face.

"I am well," Elspeth replied, catching Jorden's intent gaze once more, her brow furrowing before glancing at her lover, and giving him a reassuring kiss on the cheek.

Jorden's lips quirked.

"Can I help ye, sir?" the stable master asked, his irritation at being interrupted obvious.

"Jorden had mentioned to me that the stables had been locked, but I can see that is no longer the case."

Elspeth dropped her gaze to the ground, but Antony didn't so much as blink. "All the horses have been fed and I was not told anyone would be leaving tonight. I would be happy to assist ye now if—"

"Nay, all is well," Adelstan said, noting the concerned look in Elspeth's eyes. "Are you returning to your mistress, Elspeth?"

She swallowed hard. "I am."

"I have something to discuss with her. May I join you?"

She gave a curt nod. "Of course."

"Antony, isn't it?" Adelstan queried, and the man nodded.

"Yes, sir."

"Thank you, Antony." Adelstan glanced at Jorden. "I shall see you in the morning for drills."

Jorden perked up. "I look forward to the exercise." His gaze slid to Elspeth, who seemed amused, if not confused, by his sudden interest.

Adelstan followed behind the servant, who walked slowly and kept her shoulders erect. Hundreds of questions raced through his mind, but he knew asking Elspeth would be a waste. She would be loyal to Rhiannon and lie whenever necessary.

Nay, the person he needed to ask was probably now sitting in the tower, perhaps preparing for a bath before she climbed into bed, her body now sated.

Fury nearly choked him, almost as much as the jealousy squeezing his heart.

They made it to the tower without saying a word to each other. As they climbed the spiral staircase, Elspeth glanced back at him, but it wasn't until they reached the chamber door that she whirled around. "Ye saw her, didn't ye?"

He did his best to look confused. "Saw who?"

She frowned, and dropped her gaze to her feet. "I thought . . ."

Before he could respond, the chamber door whipped open and Rhiannon appeared, a wide smile on her face. "Elspeth, I cannot believe how wonderful that was. Thank ye so much. I shall never forget—"

All the hope Adelstan had been feeling shattered as Rhiannon's smile faded from her lips, her gaze shifting from Elspeth to Adelstan, who had stepped from the shadows.

"Adelstan, what are ye doing here?"

Adelstan put a hand on Elspeth's shoulder, and pushed her gently aside. "I would like a word alone with your mistress."

"Sir, please do not do anything ye will regret," Elspeth said, grabbing on to his tunic. "Give me your word."

He looked down at where she held a fistful of tunic, and she quickly released her hold on him.

ELEVEN

The last person Rhiannon expected to find at her chamber door, especially this time of night, was Adelstan Cawdor.

Indeed, she'd been so excited to talk to Elspeth and thank her for sharing such an intimate moment with her, that when she'd seen Adelstan, her shock must have shown tenfold.

From the look on Adelstan's face, he was not here for a friendly visit either. In fact, he looked furious.

The stable door had been locked, so no one could have known what had happened within those walls, right?

Unless someone had seen her leaving . . .

Composing herself, she walked away from the door.

Without taking his eyes from her, he stepped in and shut the door firmly behind him. A moment later he slid the bolt in place.

Her mouth went dry, and she lifted a goblet of ale with a trembling hand, bringing it to her lips.

"Explain yourself."

Setting the goblet down before she toppled it, she nervously wrung her hands together and paced before him. "What would ye like me to explain?"

"Why you, Elspeth, and Antony were in the stables behind locked doors."

Damn!

What had Elspeth told him? Already she could feel her cheeks grow hot. "I do not want to say for fear of what ye might think of me."

He ran a hand through his thick, blond hair, and she was shocked to find he trembled as well. "I can assure you that whatever you have to say cannot be worse than the images racing through my mind."

She stopped her pacing and turned to him. "What images?"

"I prefer not to say."

She stared at him for a long, awkward moment. "Oh my God, ye actually think I was with the two of them, don't ye?"

"Are you telling me you did not participate?"

"Not in the way ye are implying."

He shook his head as though he had not heard her correctly. "Then pray, tell me what you mean." He grabbed a chair, pulled it toward her, and straddled it, crossing his arms over the back. "I am all ears, my lady."

If he meant to intimidate her, he was doing one hell of a job. But even more, she found the way he sat now, his legs spread wide, his strong forearms braced over the back of the chair, sexy and masculine. He leaned forward, his light green eyes watching her closely as she paced back and forth.

"I am waiting, Rhiannon."

Taking a deep breath, she turned to face him, folding her hands demurely before her. She could see the nerve play in his jaw, the way his gaze slid over her.

She smiled inwardly. He was jealous. Jealous of what he believed had happened in that stable. What were the "images" that raced through his mind?

He cleared his throat.

"I have been curious as to what happens between a man and a woman for some time now, and since I am engaged and will be expected to share my husband's bed, I thought it wise to ask someone for assistance." Rhiannon took a deep breath, released it. "I have no mother to ask about such things, so instead I asked Elspeth to answer my many questions."

He shifted in the seat, looking increasingly uncomfortable.

"When Elspeth offered me the opportunity to watch her and Antony make love in the stables, I told her I would like to."

His green eyes narrowed. "So you watched your servant and her lover engage in sex in order to know what to expect on your wedding night?"

She met his gaze without blinking. "Aye, that is exactly what happened, whether ye choose to believe me or not. Do ye think me wicked?"

"Did this experience answer all your questions?"

"Nay."

He frowned.

"Do ye think me wicked, Adelstan?"

The corners of his mouth rose the slightest bit, and she relaxed a little. She had shocked him perhaps, but she could also see the relief in those light green eyes of his.

"I do not think you wicked, Rhiannon," he said, his voice silky soft.

Adelstan was so relieved. Nails that had been digging into the chair rail relaxed and he even managed to smile.

Rhiannon smiled in return, her chest rising and falling as she took a deep breath. The garment only reached to her ankles, showing off small, dainty feet.

As he continued to watch her, she walked toward him, this bold girl, coming to a stop not an arm's length away. He could see the outline of her pale nipples, and the triangle of hair that covered her sex. "This was not the only time I have seen two people making love." A smile played at her lips.

His cock lengthened and hardened. "If you walk around any castle, you are sure to find people making love in almost every dark alcove."

Her smile widened, a knowing grin that made the hair on the back of his neck stand on end. "Even in a bakehouse?"

He could feel blood rush to his face as her violet eyes stared into his.

She had seen him with Machara, just as he'd suspected. She had not been leaving the chapel after prayer. Rather, she had been spying on him. Perhaps intentionally.

"Your complexion has changed, Adelstan," she said, the coy smile disappearing from her angelic face.

"What I do on my own time should make little difference to you," he said, the words coming out colder than intended.

Her hands settled on her hips, pulling the material tight. He wished she wouldn't have done that, because now he could make out every detail of her beautiful body. "Why should I have to explain myself if ye do not?"

"You are to marry Baron de Cion, and he expects his bride to be chaste."

"Is *he* chaste?"

Adelstan opened his mouth and closed it as quickly.

She sighed in disgust and he noted her hands were closed into fists at her sides. "Why is it that a man can experience all lovemaking has to offer before he marries, and yet a woman is not allowed to do the same? I would be damaged goods if I slept with another, but I must accept him, a man who has been with many women, and even a wife! It is so unfair."

Pressing her lips together, she started pacing again. "I wish I had been born a man." She looked at him then, caught his gaze. "If I were a man, I would want to be as tall and strong as ye, and as handsome."

His stomach tightened.

"Ye are the perfect specimen, Adelstan. I have watched the women in this castle turn to pottage when ye come around. They begin to giggle and twitter among themselves, each vying for your attention, waiting for the moment ye notice them."

Uncomfortable with the direction the conversation had taken, Adelstan stood, and put the chair aside. "I have kept you too long. You must be tired."

"Do not leave yet," she said, the words desperate. "Please, Adelstan. I don't want ye to go."

She took a deep breath, her chest heaving as she awaited his answer.

All the blood in his body went straight to his cock.

"I do not wish to cause speculation by being with you in your chamber."

"Why are ye always worried about what others will think of ye? Why do ye care so much?"

His heart slammed against his chest as she walked toward him. "What do you mean?"

She stopped before him, and looked up, deep into his eyes. "Ye asked me earlier if watching Elspeth and Antony had answered all my questions about making love, and I told ye no, that it hadn't. Do ye know why that is?"

He shook his head, fearful of her next words.

"I want to know everything there is to know when it comes to making love. I want to make my lover happy, and please him in every way. Most women in my shoes know that a man comes to her bed, and lies with her, and that she may have a child. That is all she knows. But I know there is so much more, for I have seen it with my eyes, have watched it unfold and felt my body respond to what I was seeing."

His cock bucked and he grit his teeth at the wicked images racing in his mind.

"I know that true pleasure can be experienced when a man slips his staff into a woman's entrance," she said, running her hand down her belly, to her mons.

He swallowed hard, tried not to look at where she touched herself, but failed miserably.

"I know how to take a man's length inside my mouth and fondle his ballocks while I—"

"Rhiannon, enough," he warned, cutting her off, trying to

ignore the pulsing ache deep in his cock, and the intense fire that burned within his veins.

Her gaze shifted from his, down over his chest and belly, to the obvious ridge of his hard sex.

She reached out, touched him there with the same hand that had been on her sex just moments before. Her elegant fingers cupped his cock. He wanted to pull away. God help him he did, but his legs were like stone, much as his cock, and he couldn't move to save his life.

"*This* is what I want. To feel the very essence of your manhood in my hand." Her fingers molded around his thick length and he groaned low in his throat. "Can I feel ye, Adelstan?"

He opened his mouth to speak, and her hand moved to the cord of his braies. Warning bells rang in his head, and yet he ignored them as his braies loosened about his hips and her hand found him.

Her innocent touch was his undoing, and when she looked down at him, her violet eyes dark with desire, a wide smile on her full lips, all his willpower dissipated.

He lifted her in his arms and marched toward the bed, tossing her on the blankets that had already been turned down. She went up on her elbows, alarm on her face . . . until he reached behind his neck and pulled the tunic from his body.

Rhiannon could scarcely breathe. She had wanted this from the first moment she had set eyes on Adelstan.

His hair was mussed from pulling off his tunic, the locks falling past his broad shoulders in thick waves. He tossed the garment aside, and she stared at the wide expanse of chest, the flat, small nipples, the hard planes of his abdomen that bunched with each movement.

A familiar ache built within her, settling between her legs, making her hot and wet. She had never been so excited in all her life. She wanted this more than she'd ever wanted anything.

She scarcely blinked as he stripped off his braies, his cock jutting from his body, large and proud.

Then he was on the bed, crawling up, settling over her, his erection wedged between them. She had never experienced anything so wonderful, so beautiful, so special. Having every hard inch of his body pressed against hers sent jolts of pleasure throughout her.

His mouth covered hers, and she opened wide for him. For long minutes they just kissed, exploring each other's mouths, tasting, touching, followed by a longer, deeper kiss that had her shifting beneath him, wanting to feel him inside her.

Her hands wandered from his shoulders, down over his strong back, to his narrow waist, and the high buttocks, which she squeezed tight. He smiled against her lips and she opened her eyes to find him staring at her, his long dark lashes casting shadows on his sharp cheekbones.

So beautiful, this English warrior.

She remembered the way Elspeth had moved against Antony, and she lifted her hips against Adelstan. He smiled again, and dipped his head to kiss her. She closed her eyes, too, and enjoyed the moment, just the feel of lips against lips, tongue against tongue, heart pounding against heart.

His hands moved down her side, grazing a breast, but not stopping there. He traced her ribs, her waist, her hip, before taking the same path up again, this time stopping at her breast. His large hand covered her there, and she released a sigh.

"Ye have no idea how long I have waited for this," she whispered against his lips.

The sides of his mouth curved slowly. He pulled gently at her nipple, rolling the bud between thumb and finger. The sensations within her built by the second, a need that shot from her breasts to her wet, aching sex.

Wanting to do some exploring of her own, she urged him to roll over. Instantly, she liked the sensation of being in control, of having the freedom to touch him how she wanted.

Adelstan reached for her undertunic, and brought it up and over her head, tossing it aside. Her first reaction was to cover herself, but she stopped short of doing so, dropping her hands to his chest.

"You're so beautiful," he said, his gaze shifting to the rose-colored nipples that tipped her magnificent full breasts. The firm mounds were a perfect handful and he palmed both of them. The hair at her sex already glistened with her dew.

She was so ripe, so ready.

She touched his jaw, his neck, his chest, her fingers splaying over the wide muscle there. Her lips followed the trail her fingers had begun, and she could see and feel the hair on his arms stand on end.

Continuing downward, she kissed his flat abdomen, his navel, her tongue drawing tiny circles around and inside the small valley, before following the line of hair to the glorious cock that bucked at her attentions. The heavily veined appendage sprouted from a nest of golden hair leading to an impressive crown and a small slit where a drop of fluid had already formed.

She licked the bead from his cockhead, before her mouth closed over him.

He let out a groan that pleased her to the core. Aye, she would never forget that sound for as long as she lived.

Concentrating, she tried to mirror Elspeth's motions earlier, but knew she had much to learn.

Adelstan's blood burned within his veins. His balls were tight against his body. He would not come before he had her. He could not. They had come too far for that.

"I will not last," he said, reaching for her, pulling her up, and then flipping her over yet again, needing her beneath him just as he had envisioned a million times in recent days.

Her arms wrapped about his neck, pulling him close. He used his knees to nudge her thighs open wide. Guiding the head of his cock to her entrance, he had to grit his teeth when she lifted her hips to greet him.

He kissed her at the same time he entered her, capturing her cry with his lips. He moaned as he settled fully within her, her inner muscles cradling him like a glove, so unbelievably tight, so hot.

And then he began to move.

With each thrust, the pain subsided, followed by a pleasure that had Rhiannon eagerly meeting each stroke. One of his large hands moved down her side, reaching for her buttocks, cradling her. With the other, he touched her breast, his fingers playing with her nipple, bringing her need to a fever pitch.

He bent his head, kissed her throat and the tops of her breasts, before taking a rigid nipple into his mouth.

The dual sensations of being filled with his cock and him sucking her nipples were almost too much for Rhiannon to bear. He dropped his forehead to hers, increased his strokes, faster and faster, and she met each thrust, her fingernails digging into his shoulders.

Her heart slammed against her chest. With each thrust she came closer to orgasm, her insides tightening, her breathing increasing, and then it happened . . . her world exploded, her inner muscles squeezing him tight, taking her to a place she could only describe as paradise.

Adelstan felt the tremors clamp around his cock, pulling him in deeper. He caught Rhiannon's soft cries with his mouth, and as she held on to him, he thrust again and again. He groaned loud when his release came, pulling out of her sweet body just in time.

TWELVE

Adelstan woke up, felt the soft body beside him, and knew with a sinking feeling he had done exactly what he'd promised himself never to do.

He had made love to Rhiannon MacKay.

Malgor de Cion, and quite possibly Renaud, too, would see him swing from the highest rafters while the soldiers he had fought side by side with for over a decade applauded.

Why in God's name had he come to her chamber last night?

Because you were jealous of Antony, and you wanted to discover for yourself if she was as true and as chaste as she claimed to be.

And chaste she had been, of that he had no doubt. He had broken through her maidenhead, heard her sharp cry of pain. Last night he had found heaven in her arms, and had been stunned at the depth of the emotion he felt for her then, at that moment, when he'd looked into her incredible eyes as he made love to her.

And now, as she lay sleeping beside him, the last thing he wanted to do was leave her, but leave her he must, before day broke over the land.

Damn, what had he been thinking?

He ran a trembling hand down his face, wondering how on earth he could fix what had been done.

Removing Rhiannon's hand from his chest, he sat up and went completely still when she shifted beside him, a soft moan coming from her full lips.

He looked down at her sleeping form illuminated by the light of the moon through the small window above them, and could not help but smile. It was hard to equate the innocent sleeping beside him with the vixen in this very bed hours before.

There had been an urgency when they'd come together. An intensity he'd never before experienced. Aye, Rhiannon was the kind of lover one never got out of one's blood.

Ever.

Her eyelashes fluttered.

His heart began to pound.

She blinked a few times, focusing on him, and then the sides of her mouth curved in a shy smile. Her teeth grazed her bottom lip and he could not resist the temptation to lean down and kiss her. With a deep-throated moan, she kissed him back, looping her arms around his neck, pressing her breasts against his chest.

He felt her need, reveled in it, until a sound outside in the bailey brought him back to reality.

He pulled her hands from around his neck. "I must go, Rhiannon."

"Stay with me."

"I cannot. If your father . . ."

"He does not rise until late."

"I cannot risk being seen leaving your room in the middle of the night, not by the guard or even my own men. We would both be in a great deal of trouble."

"Would they tell de Cion?"

Hearing her betrothed's name on her lips made the blood in his veins turn to ice.

"My men are loyal to me, but I do not know how far that courtesy would extend in such circumstances. You will still marry de Cion, Rhiannon. This night will not change that, no matter how much either one of us wishes differently."

She drew away from him, pulling her knees up to her chest, hugging them to her. He saw blood on the sheets, and her gaze followed.

"Are ye surprised?" she asked, her hair falling around her like a veil. Her gaze never wavered from his and he once again reveled at her courage, at her boldness, at her spirit.

She thrilled him to the very core of his being.

Seeing the blood there, and knowing he had been the first, brought something out in him that shocked him. He didn't want to share her with anyone, least of all her future husband. But he was in an impossible situation.

"My God, ye *are* surprised." How wounded she looked.

"Nay, I am not, Rhiannon." He reached out to her but she pulled away, out of reach.

Her breasts heaved as she watched him, and his cock hardened. He ached to have her again.

"Rhiannon, I believed you when you told me the truth. I am not surprised to find you chaste. I expected as much. I have never been with a virgin before . . ."

"Truly?"

He nodded. "Truly. You are unlike any woman I have ever met. You are unique, special, and I am honored to be your first."

She stared at him, her violet eyes softening. "I want ye to be my last, too, Adelstan. Please do not tell me that we will never have another night like this one."

Swallowing past the sudden lump in his throat, he looked away from her, trying to steady his emotions. He did not want de Cion, or any other man, touching her.

"What will we do now?"

Though he wanted nothing more than to make love to her again, doing so would only endanger both of them. Standing, he gathered his clothing. "Pretend nothing has happened between us. Go on as before."

"Stolen moments," she said absently, her gaze shifting down his body. He saw the desire in her violet eyes, and the desperation, which he also felt. "That's all we shall share, isn't it, Adelstan? I will never be able to show ye any affection outside this room."

"Rhiannon, we have no choice."

She scrambled to her feet, and stood beside him a second later, naked and not at all embarrassed to be so. "I want more than that."

She had a beautiful body, all curves where they should be, high, firm breasts, flat belly. And he remembered when he had slipped into her hot core, the way her inner muscles had gripped him tight. How wet she had been, and so sexual for someone who knew very little about the ways of love.

He'd been thrilled when she had taken his cock into her mouth, tasting him.

At the memory, his cock jumped to attention. Her brow shot

up, a pleased smile on her face as she looked from his sex to his face.

Pulling all her hair over one shoulder, she took the few steps to the bed, giving him a glimpse of her naked back without the veil of hair covering her. She looked over her shoulder at him with a saucy smile.

He was on her in two strides, settling behind her, taking a handful of plump breast, pushing her feet apart to give him ample room to take her, before bending her over the bed, kissing her neck.

Rhiannon's insides tightened and her heart beat with excitement as Adelstan played with her breasts, his calloused fingers rolling her nipples, while his other hand moved down her belly to the curls that covered her sex, settling on the tiny button there.

Her breathing increased as he slipped a finger into her heated slit. He moaned loudly, the sound vibrating against her back.

His cock brushed against her buttocks, and he thrust deep into her. She gasped at how he filled her, stuffing her completely, stretching her already swollen tissues.

He slid slowly, in and out, his fingers continuing to pleasure her. The multiple sensations had her moaning in ecstasy, her fingers fisting the covers.

As she came closer to climax, she arched her back, taking him greedily, and when he increased the rhythm, a heated groan escaped her lips as she came, her sheath throbbing around his thick, long cock, coating him with her dew.

Adelstan felt the tremors of her orgasm, and continued to play with her breasts, pulling gently on her nipples, pinching them. She stood a little, and reached back to grab his ass.

His fingers brushed her clit, around it, flicking it over and over. He wanted her to come again, to remember these moments when they were apart. Her breath quickened once more, and he could no longer keep his own climax at bay. She cried out, and he felt the familiar pulsing squeeze his cock.

Adelstan's hands gripped Rhiannon's hips tight. He thrust hard against her, his sac slapping her soft folds with each stroke. He withdrew, his seed shooting onto her lower back and buttocks.

Taking the soiled sheet, he cleaned her as she lay bent over the bed, catching her breath. He smiled as she turned back to look at him, a mischievous grin on her lips.

How sated she looked, so happy, so content.

His cock still semihard, he touched her slender back, cupping her high ass possessively and placing a kiss there. She gasped with delight and turned over, her arms lifted.

He glanced at the graying sky, knew he should have left the moment he'd opened his eyes, and yet he could not pull himself away. Not this minute. Not yet. He went into her arms, kissed her with all the longing and joy he felt, pushing the guilt far away.

Rhiannon moved the food idly around her plate, trying hard to forget the events of last night. Her father had commented on the dark circles beneath her eyes, wondering what kept her up at night.

If only he knew the truth, how stunned he would be. No doubt horrified to learn his only daughter had given her maidenhead to her betrothed's fellow officer.

And the experience had been incredible. In fact, she could not help replaying the events over and over in her mind. When Adelstan had finally left after the second time they had made love, she had, with Elspeth's help, ripped the soiled linens from the bed and watched them burn in the hearth.

Rhiannon still remembered the possessiveness she'd seen in Adelstan's eyes when he'd seen the blood on the sheets, and his declaration that he had never before been with a virgin. She had wanted to ask him how many lovers he'd had, but decided she was better off not knowing.

Oddly, she felt no regret whatsoever. If she could die today, she would at least die knowing what it felt like to make love to someone she truly desired and cared about. Mayhap even loved.

"Where are the English soldiers this morning?" Deirdre asked.

Rhiannon instantly perked up, having wanted to ask the very same question herself.

Her father straightened his shoulders. "I believe they are still in drills."

"How hard they work." Deirdre's eyes widened innocently as she bit into a plum.

"Father, I would like to go to market today. Have I your permission?"

Still frowning at his wife, he merely nodded. "Take Elspeth with ye."

"Of course."

"Market?" Deirdre lifted a tawny brow. "Will ye be searching for items to take with ye to England?"

Rhiannon forced a smile she didn't feel. "Aye, I thought to perhaps find a gift for my betrothed."

Deirdre's lips thinned, while her father nodded with approval. "That is a wonderful idea, Rhiannon. I am certain Lord Malgor will be most pleased by your generosity."

Soon he would be asking her when she planned on leaving

Castle MacKay, and she would have to come up with any number of excuses why she needed to stay. Her main complaint had always been her fear of leaving Scotland and her people, a concern her father was well aware of. However, now she feared her betrothed more. Feared what her life would become once she married. Feared Adelstan leaving her once he delivered her to de Cion.

Not wanting her father or stepmother to ask her any more questions, Rhiannon stood. "Well, then, I shall be back this evening, Father. Deirdre."

Her stepmother gave a curt nod, while her father dismissed her with a wave of his hand. She ignored her half brother, who stuck his tongue out at her.

Rhiannon found Elspeth in the stables, talking to Antony, who was busy brushing down a large, white and brown speckled stallion. Her friend watched her lover with a soft expression.

Antony glanced at her. "Lady Rhiannon, how are ye this afternoon?"

"I am fine, and ye?"

"Well, thank ye."

"Elspeth, I would like to go to market."

Elspeth brightened. "Did ye ask your father?"

"Aye."

"Very well, then let's go."

"Have fun, ladies," Antony said, giving Elspeth a wink as they exited the stables.

They walked in companionable silence through the bailey and over the drawbridge. Rhiannon smoothed her skirts and looked anxiously about, hoping to see Adelstan.

Her heart gave a leap seeing in the distance a group of men, all naked to the waist, going through drills in the north meadow. She would have to walk right past them on the way to market.

Adelstan stood with his back to her, his long blond hair hanging past broad shoulders. Desire and anticipation raced through her, making her hot and moist, and aching to take up where they had left off early this morning.

"I am impressed by their devotion to physical exercise," Elspeth said, her gaze focusing on Jorden, the dark-haired warrior with silver eyes that reminded Rhiannon of a wolf's eyes.

As she and Elspeth approached, the men now stood facing each other in hand-to-hand combat. Many soldiers shot smiles their way, the devilishly handsome Jorden included, and Adelstan seeing where his soldiers' attention had been diverted, turned and put a hand up to block the sun, the motion shifting muscle beneath olive skin.

"They certainly take their duties seriously," Elspeth said, swinging her basket in hand. "Antony said they have been out since first light. I am sure their devotion comes from living in a country full of men who do not wish them there."

"And yet Adelstan is English."

"Aye, that is true. How difficult it must have been to lose everything to a foreign conqueror."

"I cannot imagine the torment he experienced."

"Nor I."

Adelstan said something to his men, and they went back to fighting, all but Jorden, who managed to get a smile in before focusing on his attacker.

"He is a handsome devil, is he not?"

Rhiannon glanced at Elspeth. "Jorden?"

"Aye," Elspeth said breathlessly. "I have heard an intriguing secret about him."

"Tell me."

Adelstan turned to look at her again, and Rhiannon feeling strangely shy, quickly looked away. She could still feel him watching her.

"Here he comes," Elspeth said anxiously.

Rhiannon's heart leapt, and when she looked up to see Adelstan walking toward her in long strides, she tried hard not to smile but could not help it. He was without a doubt the perfect male. Visions of all they had experienced last night, and what lay before them, made her blush.

Lord, what a wicked woman she had become.

His expression seemed somewhat guarded, though she caught a gleam in his green eyes. "Lady Rhiannon," he said, stopping before her. Sweat glistened off his wide chest, and she yearned to touch him there. To touch him everywhere.

"Sir Adelstan," she said, her voice sounding breathy and excited.

Elspeth watched them with a grin on her face.

"Are you off to the village?"

"A bit farther afield, actually—to market."

His brow furrowed. "How far is market?"

Rhiannon glanced at Elspeth, who replied, "Quarter of an hour journey, or so."

"Your father sends you alone?"

His concern touched her. "We have gone to market by ourselves many times, Adelstan. Isn't that right, Elspeth?"

Elspeth nodded. "Indeed, we are most capable, sir."

Adelstan's lips split into a grin as he looked from Elspeth back to Rhiannon. He glanced over his shoulder to his men, many who watched intently before going back to drills.

While his attention was elsewhere, Rhiannon let her gaze drop to the flat planes of his stomach, the muscles there bunching with the slight movement. The soft material of his braies cupped his cock.

She lifted her gaze just in time.

"My men have been at it long enough. I shall escort you myself. You are my charge, after all."

Pleased and excited he had decided to join them, Rhiannon nodded. "Very well. We shall wait for ye at the end of the village beside the old Roman wall."

"I will see you soon." With a nod, he walked off, and she watched his retreating form, the broad shoulders that came down to a vee at his narrow waist, the high curve of his ass, and the long legs.

She heard a few of his men laugh, and wondered if she had been caught staring.

Elspeth took her by the hand. "Come, let's go."

Rhiannon felt like dancing.

"He truly is a gorgeous man, Rhiannon."

"Aye, he is. I never thought I would feel this way, Elspeth. Not ever. I don't want to go to Almeron. I can't bear the thought of marrying a stranger now. How can I allow anyone else to touch me that way?"

Elspeth squeezed her hand. "Do not fret over what ye cannot control, Rhiannon. I'm not in any hurry to leave either, and yet I know the day is coming."

"Will ye miss Antony?"

She nodded. "Of course. It will hurt to leave, and yet there is a part of me that is excited about the future."

"Ye say that only to ease my fears."

"Nay, I say it because I mean it. I have lived here all my life.

Will I miss the castle and its people? Of course I shall, but I am most anxious to meet new people, and to see something besides these familiar lochs and hills. I even heard one of the English soldiers say that it is not as cold in England."

"Now that is a blessing."

"Indeed, it is."

They quieted as they walked into the village, nodding to those they passed.

"Ye mentioned earlier about hearing something intriguing regarding Jorden."

"Aye," Elspeth said, stopping in midstep. "But ye must keep what I tell ye to yourself."

"Of course I will keep it to myself."

Elspeth looked over both shoulders. Satisfied no one could hear, she said, "Antony told me he walked into the stables and found Jorden and another Norman knight." She lifted her brows nearly to her hairline. "Together."

Rhiannon frowned. "Perhaps they were attending to their horses?"

Elspeth's eyes widened a little. "Rhiannon, I do not mean they were together as friends. They were together, as in kissing and—well, doing what lovers do."

Rhiannon gasped.

"I know! Antony could not believe his eyes. Indeed, the younger knight's cheeks turned crimson red, but Jorden did not even bat an eye. In fact, he pulled the younger man's face back to his, and kissed him passionately."

"But he is so—handsome—"

"Oh, my dearest Rhiannon," Elspeth said with a laugh. "Ye have so much to learn of the world around ye. I know we are all born to believe that intimate relationships involve one man and one woman, and yet, that is not how it is."

Rhiannon had a difficult time digesting the information, especially since she had seen the way Jorden looked at Elspeth. "I am not so innocent that I didn't believe such relationships existed. I just never thought someone like Jorden . . ."

"Say nothing to no one, because I do not want it getting back to Jorden or Adelstan." Her grin deepened. "Although I get the impression Jorden would not care if the whole world knew where his passions lie."

Rhiannon bit her bottom lip. "Aye, he is a cocky one to be sure."

"Do you speak of me, Lady Rhiannon?"

THIRTEEN

Rhiannon's heart nearly leapt from her chest as she looked up to find Adelstan astride his horse, his brow lifted inquisitively as he awaited her answer.

Ironically, beside him was the very man she and Elspeth had been discussing.

"Nay, we were discussing a guard," she blurted out, in way of a quick answer.

"A cocky guard?"

"Aye." Her gaze shifted to Jorden to find him staring back at her, his silver eyes intense. He inclined his head the slightest bit and she nodded in return, her cheeks turning hot as she thought of him kissing another man.

Strangely, the idea was not altogether offensive.

Elspeth looked surprised, and strangely excited that the handsome knight had joined them. "We thought we would ride in case you decided to purchase more items at market than we could carry."

"A wise choice," Elspeth said, swinging the basket she carried.

Both men dismounted and helped Rhiannon and Elspeth onto the horses. Rhiannon winced as her aching tissues made contact with the horse's back. Indeed, she ached in more than one place today.

Adelstan settled behind her, and Rhiannon rested her back against his hard chest, enjoying the intimate contact. Her heart rate accelerated as she remembered details of their night together.

"Were you really speaking of a guard?" he asked, his voice hinting at jealousy.

She would not lie to him. "Nay."

"Then who?" His breath stirred the hair at her neck.

She nodded toward Jorden, who was laughing at something Elspeth had said.

"Your complexion changed when you looked at Jorden, so I thought that might be the case."

She wasn't about to tell him the real reason behind her blush.

"He is my friend, but I will fight him for your affection if I must."

She looked back at him and saw he was grinning. "Ye have nothing to be concerned about. I fancy ye, Adelstan, and only ye." She stared straight into his green eyes, letting him know she spoke the absolute truth.

"I am glad to hear it. I have been thinking of you all morning."

His words pleased her immensely. "I've been thinking of ye all morning, too."

His hands rested on either side of her hips, and he leaned his head down and kissed the top of her head, breathing deeply. "You smell wonderful. Like several different scents combined."

"I use oils in my bathwater."

He groaned, a wonderful sound that came deep from his chest.

"Did I say something wrong?"

"Nay, I was just imagining you taking a bath."

She smiled.

His eyes danced.

Checking to see that Elspeth and Jorden were now but a dot on the horizon, Rhiannon reached up and cupped Adelstan's strong jaw and kissed him. He surprised her by deepening the kiss, his tongue darting past her lips, stroking hers. He tasted of mint, sweet and delicious.

She felt the hard ridge of his sex pressed against her hip and smiled. She yearned to be alone with him again, where they could explore each other's bodies.

He reached up, between the edges of her cloak, and touched her breast, his fingers gentle as he pulled at the sensitive bud. Just like last evening, her body responded in kind, and it felt as if an invisible string were connected from her breasts to her sex.

"I want you again," he said against her ear. "I'll never get enough of you."

His gruff words pleased her more than he would ever know. "I want ye, too."

He touched her between her legs, brushing his fingers over her hidden pearl. She shifted as he used his tongue to trace the outline of her ear. Her breathing increased, as did the pressure building within her. His cock felt like marble against her back. How she ached to ride him.

The sounds of market pierced the quiet, bringing them both back to the present. Normally Rhiannon looked forward to market, but now she wanted only to be alone with Adelstan, to continue what he had started. His hands returned to the reins again, leaving her aching for his touch.

They crested the final hill to the market itself, and Rhiannon smiled while inhaling deeply of herbs and fresh-picked flowers.

Jorden was in the process of dismounting, a young boy from the village holding on to the reins, his free hand out for coin. Elspeth let her hand linger on the knight's forearm and Rhiannon wondered what her friend was up to.

Adelstan's lips brushed her ear. "Why do you stare at my officer, Rhiannon?" Though he smiled, there was a vulnerability in his green eyes that surprised her.

"I think Elspeth likes him."

"Ah," he said, grinning boyishly. "Is that the only reason?"

"What other reason would there be?"

"Mayhap you desire him, too."

"The only man I desire is with me now."

His eyes searched hers, and she knew he wanted to touch her as badly as she wanted to touch him. "You know exactly what to say to unman me."

She smiled. "I'm glad."

Before he could say a word, she slid from the horse, and waited for him to dismount. Elspeth waved and flashed a saucy grin before taking Jorden by the hand, leading him into the marketplace.

"I like your maid," Adelstan said, brushing his hand against hers as they walked side by side. "She is loyal to you."

"Aye, she is. I trust her with my life."

Rhiannon wished more than anything they could walk hand in hand like two lovers, but that was impossible.

"Lady Rhiannon," Gerard's grandmother said, waving at her from her stand where she sold eggs, butter, and cheese.

Waving to the woman, Rhiannon felt a sickening feeling in the pit of her stomach. She had completely forgotten about Gerard, the boy she'd had a crush on for so long now. How ironic that since Adelstan had come into her life, she had scarcely thought of the young man.

As they walked, she could feel others watching them. None frowned or looked at her in an accusing way, but she still felt nervous.

"My lady, we have fresh lavender today," another yelled out.

"I shall purchase some before I leave, Mariam. I am running low."

"Wonderful, my lady. I shall prepare a bushel for you."

Adelstan walked beside her, his hands clasped behind his back, a smile on his face. "It is a good thing Jorden and I brought the horses."

She laughed under her breath. "Actually, oftentimes we send a wagon and one of the kitchen staff to collect the items."

His lips quirked. "Ah, I see."

"I did not want to disappoint ye."

"You could not disappoint me." She could clearly see the desire in his eyes.

Her heart missed a beat and she looked away, and straight at Gerard, who instantly brightened.

The young man hadn't noticed Adelstan, or mayhap he had not paid any attention, until now. The smile on his lips faltered for only a moment as his gaze shifted between her and her escort. "Lady Rhiannon, how are ye this fine morning?"

"I am very well, thank you, Gerard. And ye?"

He ran a hand through his thick hair. "I am well, though I understand ye shall be leaving us soon, Lady Rhiannon."

Could she not escape her future anywhere? She nodded. "Indeed, I will be, but ye are not rid of me yet, Gerard. I hope to stay on for a while longer."

He grinned, showing deep dimples. "I am glad to hear it, Lady Rhiannon."

"I shall return in a moment," Adelstan said, and she nodded, watching from the corner of her eye as he walked across the way to a produce stand, where he immediately struck up a conversation with Clarence, an old farmer.

Rhiannon reached out and touched the fine carving on a pendant, one of the wares Gerard and his grandfather sold at their booth.

She was shocked when Gerard's fingers covered hers. "I shall miss ye, Lady Rhiannon. Most desperately."

His words made her uneasy, almost as much as the look of passion in his eyes. She knew that look, understood it with a realization that made her stomach knot.

She looked at where his hand still rested on hers. He instantly dropped his hand to his side. "Forgive me. I did not mean—"

"I shall miss ye, too, Gerard." She smiled, hoping to put him at ease. "Ye have been a dear friend to me, and I hope one day when I return to visit, that ye will have found a lovely young woman who is worthy of ye."

A sad smile came over his face.

She glanced over her shoulder to find Adelstan in deep conversation with Clarence, and also noticed Jorden and Elspeth over by the minstrels. "Gerard, I have a favor to ask of ye," she said, lowering her voice. "This is extremely important to me, and I can ask no one else, because I trust ye more than anyone else here."

His brows furrowed. "Of course, my lady. Anything."

"I would like ye to make me a ring."

"For ye?"

"Nay, a man's ring."

"For your intended?"

She nodded and removed the parchment from her pocket. "It is a simple rendering, but I trust ye can make sense of it."

"Perhaps my grandfather would be a better choice? After all, I have only been an ap—"

"I want *ye* to make it, Gerard," she said firmly. "Please."

"I am honored to do so for ye."

"I would like ye to add the following inscription to the inside of the band."

Her cheeks turned hot as he read, "*Gra Gael Mo Chroi, R,*" which meant *love of my heart* in Gaelic. Gerard's eyes widened. "He is a lucky man," he said, carefully folding the parchment and placing it in the small pouch at his waist.

"How long will it take ye?"

"I could have it finished by next week."

"Perfect."

"Ye have my word, my lady. I shall not speak about this to anyone, not even my grandparents."

"Thank ye, Gerard. I knew I could trust ye."

Turning, she nearly ran straight into Adelstan's wide chest. He was eating an apple, and he offered her one.

She shook her head. "I already ate this morning while you were out on drills."

"Ah," he said, offering the fruit to Gerard, who also declined it.

Adelstan pocketed the fruit. As they walked away from Gerard's stand, he bent his head and whispered, "The boy fancies you, Rhiannon."

"He is a good friend."

"A friend?"

"Aye."

He frowned a little, as though he did not quite believe her, then took another bite of the apple. Juice wetted his lips as he chewed.

Her belly tightened, and desire made the blood in her veins burn. Even the slight friction between her thighs made her hot and wet for him, and her nipples rubbed against her chemise.

Remembering where they were and that they had an audience, she tore her gaze away and continued to walk, taking in everything, knowing soon she may never see these people again.

Three women sat together, working on tapestries, one an image of Castle MacKay, and she stopped in her tracks. It was not the best rendering she had seen, but she liked the woman's use of colors.

"Lady Rhiannon," the older of the women said, nodding her head in greeting. The other two women, both younger than Adelstan and older than herself, looked at Adelstan with interest. The bolder and more voluptuous of the two, a beautiful blonde Rhiannon had noticed on several occasions, never once dropped her gaze as she smiled.

Adelstan returned the smile, and Rhiannon had the urge to elbow him.

Perhaps the one thing she should be grateful for was the fact that, once she married, he would not be staying at Almeron for long, and therefore she would not have to endure a lifetime of other women staring at him, wanting him, flirting with him right in front of her.

However, she hated being reminded that Adelstan did not belong to her, nor would he ever.

"Do ye like it, sir?" the blonde asked, standing, and Rhiannon wondered if she referred to the tapestry or to herself.

It didn't help that the woman's kirtle looked a size or two too small for her voluptuous frame.

"I do like it. It is most impressive."

Impressive? The woman or the tapestry?

Good lord, why had she stopped to look at their wares?

She felt compelled to take Adelstan by the hand and lead him away, but to do so would look sad and childish, and cause speculation she could not afford.

"Would ye like the tapestry in memory of Castle MacKay, Lady Rhiannon?" the blonde asked, her gaze shifting once again to Adelstan. "Mayhap I can bring it to the castle myself this evening?"

Rhiannon prayed the jealousy boiling over within her did not show on her face. "Nay, to have such a tapestry would only make me sad and miss home," she lied, glad to see the blonde's smile turn into a frown. "Ye are very talented. Your rendering of Castle MacKay was very accurate."

The woman beamed at Rhiannon.

No wonder most men found women so easy to manipulate. A kind smile or remark and they were as soft as hot wax in one's hands. "Good day, ladies."

"Good day, Lady Rhiannon," they said in unison.

Rhiannon started walking, not even waiting for Adelstan. It was ridiculous to be angry with him. He couldn't help how women reacted to him . . . he just didn't need to enjoy the attention so much.

Seeing Elspeth and Jorden, she approached them, noting the flower in her maid's hand. Apparently the knight had a flair for the romantic.

Jorden glanced past her to Adelstan. "Elspeth had a wonderful idea. She thought mayhap we should buy a few items and have our own feast, out under the sky."

Rhiannon wondered if perhaps Antony had been wrong about Jorden and the young knight being lovers, for he seemed very aware of women. Perhaps he had made it up hoping Elspeth would be put off by the story. If so, it had the opposite effect, for Elspeth appeared completely enamored of the charming knight.

"That sounds like a wonderful idea," Adelstan said, taking the apple from his pocket and tossing it to Jorden. "Where are you thinking of having such a feast?"

"Someplace private," Elspeth said with a smile.

FOURTEEN

The moment they were out of sight of the village, Adelstan's arm wrapped possessively around Rhiannon's waist, but only for a moment before taking hold of the reins.

Ahead of them Jorden and Elspeth kissed, and Rhiannon smiled back at Adelstan. If only she could be so bold and open with her feelings, she would kiss him now, uncaring of who saw them. But they did not have the same luxury as their friends. No one must know the true nature of their relationship. She had taken a chance leaving the parchment with the inscription with Gerard, and she trusted him to show no one. If anyone were to find out, specifically her father, she would have to convince him the ring had been commissioned for de Cion.

"You are so quiet," Adelstan whispered in her ear, his lips touching the ridge, sending shivers up her spine.

"Am I?"

"What are you thinking about?"

"Ye."

She looked into his eyes and his gaze searched hers. A strange melancholy washed over her, and it was all she could do not to cry.

"Was it the women back at the market?"

"Nay, I just hate that I must hide how I feel toward ye to everyone. I want to touch ye so desperately—something as simple as holding your hand, and yet I cannot." Her gaze lowered to his lips. "I want to kiss ye—something other lovers take for granted, and I cannot."

He lowered his mouth and kissed her, his lips soft and gentle. For a moment she allowed herself the luxury of responding, until she remembered they were not alone.

She pulled away, and looked to Jorden and Elspeth, who were too wrapped up in their own little world to notice.

"Jorden would die before he betrayed me," Adelstan said, his eyes intense, as he pressed his palm to her cheek.

"And Elspeth would die before she betrayed me."

His thumb brushed along her lower lip. "Then let's enjoy this day for what it is."

Finding an isolated spot in which to have their feast, Rhiannon and Elspeth went about setting out the items for the men to devour, and devour they did.

Adelstan rested on his side, propped up on an elbow, eating the last of the cheese. Rhiannon sat across from him, watching him beneath lowered lids. God, but he was gorgeous. So much so, he took the breath from her lungs. Every time their eyes met, his lips would curve into a soft smile.

How she ached to be with him again.

Elspeth laughed at something Jorden said, and brushed a leaf from his hair, her fingers lingering long after the leaf had been discarded. The knight moved so his head rested in her lap, and Rhiannon admired her friend for her ability to tie men around her finger so easily. Jorden reached up, pulled her face down to meet his, and the two began kissing.

Rhiannon knew it was rude to watch, but she could not help it. Feeling Adelstan's stare, she looked up and her heart lurched. He wanted her with the same intensity she wanted him.

Jorden stood, and reached out to take Elspeth's hand. Rhiannon could see the surprise in her friend's eyes, but also the excitement.

"We are going for a walk down by the pond," Jorden said over his shoulder.

"How long will you be?" Adelstan asked.

Elspeth looked at Rhiannon. "An hour."

Adelstan smiled. "We shall see you when you return. Have a nice swim."

Elspeth watched Jorden undress, uncovering each inch of his powerful body to her all-consuming gaze. Since Antony had told her about him kissing the soldier, she'd been unable to purge the handsome knight from her thoughts.

Obviously he had no preference when it came to sex, because no one could fake the passion she saw in those long-lashed, silver eyes. She had never been with such a strong man, a warrior, and her heart accelerated knowing what was to come.

Naked now, he walked toward the pond, and she stared at his backside, the muscles shifting with each movement, his high firm ass and lovely strong thighs, making her pulse quicken.

Lifting her skirts to her thighs, she followed him, and stepped into the pond, her toes squishing into the sand and silt beneath her feet. Though she was far from modest, she was a bit self-conscious about being naked in front of a man she had literally met mere hours before.

Jorden dove under the water and she watched expectantly as he came up a minute later, flipping his hair out of his face, and grinning in a way that made her bones turn to butter.

Sweet Jesus, but the man was sexy, and he was walking toward her, uncaring that with each step he revealed more skin . . . his wide chest, the rippling mass of abdominal muscles, the trail of dark hair that led to his impressive cock.

The cool water did little to lessen his girth or length, or if it did, she was in trouble. Water sluiced down his body, making droplets on his olive skin. Droplets she craved to lick off. His confidence intimidated her, and yet excited her in a way she'd never before experienced.

He stopped mere inches from her and, without saying a word, leaned in for a kiss. His hands were at her back, untying the lacings of her kirtle, which he made quick work of, surprising her yet again. This man was no stranger to unlacing a woman's gown.

The kirtle was up and off her head before she could blink, and her chemise shortly followed.

Her stomach coiled. She stood before him naked as could be in the bright light of day. Because of her station in life, and having to be with Rhiannon nearly every minute of the day, she had become accustomed to making love quickly before returning to her charge, which meant rarely undressing, and when she did, it was rarely during the day.

Jorden acted as if they had all the time in the world. She trembled when he took a step back, his eyes sliding down her body slowly. The side of his mouth curved, and he grabbed her, his mouth on hers, his hand at the back of her head, fisting her hair.

Exhilaration licked her spine, and her already moist core grew wet in an instant. He rubbed his cock against her belly, his teeth biting into her bottom lip as he sucked it hard, his hand sliding down her stomach, through the hair on her mons, to her slick folds.

He released a growl as one finger, then another slid into her moist heat, his thumb brushing over her clit, first softly, and then with more pressure.

Aye, he had been with a woman before—and more than once.

Planting a hand on his wide chest, she tried to steady herself on legs that had gone weak and wobbly. As the rhythm of his fingers increased, she touched his nipple, smiling as it extended. He groaned low in his throat when she replaced her fingers with her mouth, playing with the bud and feeling the hard ridge of his sex buck against her in response.

She was lifted off the ground a second later, and laid down on soft grass. Jorden covered her with his large body, kissing her, before going up on his knees and hooking both her legs over his shoulders. He rested the crown of his cock against her wet opening, and turned his head to kiss the inside of her knee before slipping inside her.

His hands curled around her thighs as he slowly pumped in and out of her, his balls slapping her ass with each hard thrust. She released the breath she hadn't realized she'd been holding.

He said something in French she didn't understand, but it

sounded lovely, his eyes soft as he watched her, his gaze shifting to her breasts, which bounced with each hard thrust.

Long strands of wet hair stuck to his neck and shoulders, beads of water falling onto her thighs, rolling down to mingle with the creamy honey of her sex.

He slowed a little, positioning her so the head of his cock touched her sweet spot inside. It felt delicious, so incredible. He slid a long finger into her back passage and she released a sigh, biting the inside of her lip as her body rocked with pleasure.

Unable to help herself, she touched her clit, drawing circles around the tiny nub, before applying more pressure.

Jorden's jaw clenched as he watched Elspeth play with herself, his strokes increasing as she came closer to orgasm. He knew she was close, could feel her legs tighten against his shoulders.

He added another finger in her ass, and she cried out as she came, her fingers pressing harder as she rode out the sensations, her strong inner muscles throbbing around his great length.

She opened her eyes to find him watching her with an openmouthed expression that looked almost boyish. Her hand slipped from her tiny button, to fondle his balls, finding the patch of skin that made most men come immediately.

Jorden was no exception.

He moaned, the cords of his neck strained as he pumped into her hard. His silver eyes stayed focused on her, so intense. His fingernails dug into her thighs as he let out a growl and withdrew, his hot semen shooting onto her belly.

"You are being quiet again."

Rhiannon glanced up at Adelstan. All day she had been wondering how she would live with the fact he would be unmarried and free to do what he desired, while she would be married, her every moment accounted for by a man she did not even know, and had no desire to know, for that matter.

Just like her mother.

Perhaps they could run away.

"Come here," he said, pulling her into his arms, lying back on his mantle, which had been spread out, the food now forgotten.

Tears that had burned the backs of her eyes finally escaped and slipped down her cheeks.

He took her face in his hands, brushing at her tears with his thumbs, his eyes full of concern. "What is it?"

"I have realized how impossible our situation is."

He opened his mouth as though to say something, but closed it as quickly. Sitting up, he reached for the wine, took a long drink. She watched the muscles of his throat contract, her heart racing as his gaze met hers over the bottle's edge. Setting the bottle aside, he grabbed her and kissed her long and hard.

She returned the kiss fervently, needing him as much as he needed her, if not more. Her fingers wove through his hair, and she tugged at it in her urgency. He smiled against her lips, apparently pleased by her response.

He flipped, so she was now beneath him, and he drew up her skirts, his long fingers grazing the sensitive skin of her inner calf, her knee, her thighs. Disappearing beneath her skirts, his hot breath fanned against her sex a moment before his tongue licked her heated cleft.

Her heart nearly pounded out of her chest as he licked her mercilessly, his tongue lifting the small hard bud, before his mouth closed over it and he sucked.

She smiled at blue skies overhead, and arched her hips closer to his mouth.

Long fingers joined the play, sliding into her hot core, and she moaned as he moved them in and out of her. He slid a finger over her back passage, and she jerked, shocked by the strange sensations.

She thought she heard the rumblings of laughter against her sex, before he once again set to laving and sucking. Liquid fire danced in her veins and her body pulsed with the familiar stirrings, the introduction to a climax that would be exquisite. Two more strokes of his tongue and a thrust of his fingers and she came hard, her inner muscles clamping around him, coating him with her juices.

As she recovered from the orgasm, he slid from beneath her skirts, his cock hard and long, tenting the braies he was busy untying. Pushing the breeches to his knees, he went into her arms, his body covering hers, his rock-hard cock resting against her still-throbbing quim.

"I want you, Rhiannon," he whispered, kissing her, the scent of her on his lips and in his mouth. She knew some women might be repulsed at tasting themselves on their lover's lips, but not Rhiannon. She wished to experience everything with this man.

"I want ye, too."

He thrust hard, burying his length inside her.

The world around them could have caught fire and she would not have known, too intent on the man staring at her, moving above her, filling her completely with his thick cock, his thrusts steady and long.

She could see the pulse racing in his neck, the way the tendons flexed. Never would she forget this moment, staring into his eyes as he made love to her. As the stirrings of yet another climax began, she brought her legs up, her feet locking behind his back, taking him deeper within her body.

"Rhiannon," he said, his strokes becoming faster.

He grabbed her ass with both hands and drove into her in shallow strokes.

As she cried out his name, he pumped a few more times and withdrew, spilling his seed onto the ground beneath her with a curse.

What would it feel like to have him come inside her—to enjoy the climax together, just once?

He stood and helped her up, kissing her thoroughly before looking anxiously around. Every moment had to be guarded and she hated it. He covered his spent seed with dirt and leaves, and pulled up his braies.

"You've dirt on your back," he said, brushing at her bottom, the sensation sending pleasure through her. If only she could stay here all day, experiencing heaven in his arms.

"Jorden!" Elspeth yelled loudly in the distance, and Rhiannon knew it was her maid's way of giving her fair warning. Thankful, she brushed her skirts out, picked up Adelstan's mantle, and tossed it to him as she made busy putting the few uneaten items into the basket.

Elspeth raced into the clearing first, looking at Rhiannon and Adelstan, almost doing a check before turning to Jorden, who appeared to have gone swimming, his dark hair wet and curling at his shoulders. "You run fast for a woman," he said, his French accent rife with sexual tension.

"Of course I do when a predator is after me," she said saucily.

"Who do you call a predator, woman?"

"Are you two quite finished?" Adelstan said with a smile, while fastening the mantle over his broad shoulders.

Jorden's silver eyes burned into Elspeth. "For now."

Elspeth's eyes widened and she laughed as she took the basket from Rhiannon.

"I can take it."

"Nay, it is heavy," Elspeth insisted, and Rhiannon let the basket slip from her fingers as the servant took it.

Jorden approached Elspeth and she rushed away, with him racing after her.

Adelstan smiled as he watched the two, before looking at Rhiannon. She returned his smile and he kissed her, a quick peck on the lips. "You're so beautiful, Rhiannon. I'll never forget these days for the rest of my life."

"Nor will I."

Jorden had Elspeth's back flush against a tree, the basket now forgotten at their feet.

The man towered over her, bending his head for a kiss. Elspeth trembled and Rhiannon wondered if it came from fear or desire.

As the maid's hands laced around the knight's shoulders, Rhiannon had her answer. There was nothing gentle about the kiss the two shared, and she had to wonder what had transpired at the pond to make his need so great.

"Come, let us leave them," Adelstan said, taking her hand within his own.

"I want to see ye tonight," she said, leaning her head against his shoulder.

"It is too risky, especially if we have been out all day together."

"I could sneak to your room."

He stopped in midstride, pulled her behind a giant oak. "I

want nothing more than to spend the entire night in your arms and wake there, and yet to do so could risk both our lives."

Disappointed, she looked down at the ground between them.

He lifted her chin with gentle fingers. "Rhiannon, if I could change this, I would. Do you believe that?"

Unable to speak for fear her voice would break, she nodded.

FIFTEEN

Two nights later Rhiannon was desperate to be alone with Adelstan again. He'd been out on a hunt with her father and his men, and they had all just returned to the hall to a great feast and dancing.

All day Rhiannon had been preparing for this evening, and her heart raced as she stepped into the bailey, the music from the great hall filling the night air, sending a rush of excitement through her entire body.

She brushed out the skirts of her new kirtle, a lovely blue material that hugged her slender frame. The silver girdle complimented the detailed embroidery at the neck and cuffs, and she'd driven Elspeth half crazy, having her style her hair over and over again.

Taking a calming breath, she entered the hall, her gaze going to the high dais and the tall blond sitting to her father's right. To her chagrin, Machara, the bold servant, was lingering nearby, washbowl at the ready.

Damn that woman!

Rhiannon stopped for a moment to talk with several friends, trying with difficulty not to look at Adelstan.

But she could feel his green gaze burning into her.

If only she could read his thoughts. Did he yearn for her in the same way she yearned for him? Even now she felt the familiar stirring in her breasts and between her thighs. Each night he filled her dreams, and each day she could think of nothing but seeing him again.

And now since days had passed without touching him, she ached to make love to him again.

A page helped her up the steps to the dais, and both her father and Adelstan stood.

"There you are, my dear," her father said with a welcome smile. "How lovely ye look this evening. Is that a new gown?"

"Thank ye, Father. Yes, it is a new gown."

His gaze fell on her hair, and he quirked his lips but said nothing.

"How was your hunt?" she asked, looking at Adelstan. Her heart leapt at seeing heat in his eyes.

"Successful." Adelstan looked to her father. "I think it is safe to say Castle MacKay's kitchens will be stocked with enough venison to keep the people happy for a long time to come."

She was greatly impressed with other skills he possessed as well.

"Indeed," she said, moving to pass by her father, but motioned toward the place to his left. "Your stepmother is not feeling well this evening, so she will be staying in our chamber. I would like ye to take her place so that we may converse."

Disappointment ate at her insides. "Of course, Father."

Throughout supper, Rhiannon bit her lip several times, especially when Machara came around, lingering before Adelstan, who did nothing to encourage her that Rhiannon could see.

Still, jealousy made her grit her teeth a time or two.

Not only that, she could see the women at the tables below watching him. What would she do when they reached Almeron and she discovered he had a leman there, or someone special to him? There would be naught she could do to stop him from being with anyone else.

Nothing.

She had no hold on him now, and when she married, all hope would be lost.

Lifting the goblet to her lips, she took a long drink of the hearty ale, enjoying the way it warmed her belly. She caught sight of Elspeth below, her attention shifting between Adelstan and Rhiannon. Their gazes caught and Rhiannon could see the sympathy in her friend's eyes.

Such a hopeless situation.

"I spoke to Elspeth earlier today and she said ye had not yet packed."

Her stomach twisted. "I am not ready to leave, Father."

His eyes narrowed and he forced a smile. "It is expected that ye will mourn leaving Castle MacKay and your family, but this is your duty, Rhiannon. Postponing the trip will only make your betrothed question if ye want this marriage or not."

"No one ever asked me if I wanted this marriage, Father."

He lifted a brow, his expression set in stone. "Ye are my daughter and ye do as I say. Ye will marry Lord Malgor for your family and for your people."

"And what of my wishes, Father? Not once have ye asked me how I felt about this marriage."

"Lower your voice, Daughter."

From the corner of her eye, she could see Adelstan sitting back in his chair, no doubt listening to every word.

"Once I leave Castle MacKay, I will never return, and ye ask me why I am so hesitant to leave?" She folded trembling hands together.

"Lord Malgor is anxious to marry ye, and ye should show him the same courtesy. Your place is at his side."

The only reason de Cion was anxious to marry her was for her dowry and to get her with child. She was a pawn, plain and simple, and she bit her lip lest she tell her father just that.

She lifted her chin and straightened her shoulders. "Be that as it may, I am not ready to leave Scotland yet, Father."

"I know ye love your home, and I enjoy having ye here, but ye will not be so far that I cannot see ye from time to time."

"Ye have not left Castle MacKay for a decade, Father. Ye will not be coming to England to see me, and I am certain I shall be too busy with my duties as Lady of Almeron to return to Scotland."

"It is true I have not left my home. I find comfort within these walls."

"As do I."

He swallowed hard and looked away, but not before she saw the frustration in his eyes. Adelstan was busy eating pheasant from the trencher, but she knew he hung on every word.

"I would like ye to consider leaving within a fortnight."

It was more than she had been hoping for, and yet her heart said, *Too soon.*

"Rhiannon, I must insist." Her father's voice held a hint of impatience.

"Yes, Father. A fortnight and no more." She took yet another drink and sat back in her chair.

"Good." Standing, her father clapped his hands twice and the minstrels began to play. Rhiannon glanced over at Adelstan, but he did not look at her once.

She knew he had to have heard their conversation, and perhaps that was why he refused to look at her. How did he feel having heard the news firsthand?

Rhiannon finished her ale, and a page was quick to refill it. By the time she swallowed the last drop, the hall had been cleared and dancers filled the floor. Laughter and music rose up to the high, timbered ceiling, and Rhiannon wanted only to find a quiet place where she could be alone with Adelstan.

Jorden approached the high table, and bowed before her father. "May I have the honor of dancing with your lovely daughter, Laird MacKay?"

Her father smiled, looking pleased by the request. "Of course." He nodded to Rhiannon, who stood on unsteady legs. Perhaps she had drunk far too much.

She felt Adelstan's gaze on her as she took Jorden's hand and he led her toward the other dancers. "You look stunning this evening, my lady," he whispered near her ear, his breath smelling of sweet wine.

"Thank ye, and ye are very handsome."

He flashed a grin that made her pulse skip a beat. She could see why women, and men, found him attractive. His dark good looks and wickedly gorgeous eyes could not be ignored, but then again, nor could Adelstan's light good looks.

The music began and Rhiannon focused on the moves of the

dance, hoping she looked relaxed and fluid. She glanced at Adelstan once to find him staring at her, his expression indecipherable.
He spoke with one of his knights, an attractive light-haired young
man who watched Jorden closely.

Was this Jorden's mystery lover?

"Lady Rhiannon, would you be so kind as to relay a message to
your maid for me?"

Elspeth had been in a wonderful mood since the day they had
visited the market and Rhiannon need not wonder why.

"Certainly, but perhaps ye wish to relay it yourself since she is
sitting very near."

"I would, but a certain man has been lingering at her side all
night. I do not think he would appreciate my interrupting."

So Antony had taken notice of the two?

"Very well, I shall relay any message ye wish."

"Tell her I shall be delighted to meet her in the brewhouse
storage this evening directly after the festivities."

Rhiannon's surprise must have shown on her face, for he laughed
under his breath. "You blush, my lady. Have I offended you?"

"Nay," she said, a touch too quickly. "My maid is plain speaking herself, so I do not pretend to guess at the extent of your
relationship, especially when ye are meeting in the brewhouse
storage."

"Point taken, my lady." The dance took them away for a few
counts, and it gave her time to collect her thoughts. Elspeth talked
with Antony, who toyed with a lock of her hair. She swatted at his
hand, and he laughed at her.

Rhiannon had noticed the stable master speaking with another servant, even pinching her bum the way he'd been pinching

Elspeth's, so perhaps their relationship was more casual than Rhiannon had ever realized.

When the dance brought them face to face again, Jorden asked, "Tell me, has the stable boy been Elspeth's lover long?"

Her heart leapt at the direct question. "Ye are asking the wrong person, and by the way, he is the stable master."

He laughed under his breath. "It is not in my nature to be jealous, Lady Rhiannon, if that is what concerns you."

"I do not know why ye should be concerned with her relationship when ye yourself have another lover." The moment the words were out, she wished to take them back, but it was too late.

His silver eyes narrowed a little and yet the smile remained. "Ah, I see the stable *boy* has been talking."

Her cheeks turned hot. "Perhaps he has."

"Does what he said surprise you?"

Stunned at his openness to discuss intimate details, she shrugged.

He laughed lightly. "Ah, I can see by the blush on your cheeks, it does." Leaning in, he whispered in her ear, "One cannot help who one is attracted to."

His good humor was contagious, and she found herself smiling, too. Or perhaps it was the ale, she knew not which. But she liked the charming knight.

"Well, let me say this while I have you to myself. Lord Malgor is a lucky man to have such a woman as you for his bride. I pray you find love for him, and he with you."

She forced the smile to stay on her lips. Apparently he had not guessed at the extent of her relationship with Adelstan. "Thank ye, Jorden."

"You are most welcome."

The last strings of the music quieted, and Jorden bowed. "Thank you for the dance, Lady Rhiannon."

"Thank ye, Jorden. I shall relay your message as soon as I am able."

"Thank you."

Seeing Elspeth and Antony still conversing, Rhiannon walked toward the high dais and stopped short seeing Adelstan approach.

"Can I have the next dance, my lady?"

"Of course," she said, trying to contain her happiness. Her heart fluttered uncontrollably as she took his hand. She loved his scent. Knew she would never forget it. How she ached to press against him, to feel his body against hers, to taste his lips. She leaned closer and whispered, "I miss ye so much."

"And I you."

The music began and their gazes locked and held.

I want to be alone with ye tonight.

How she longed to say those words but didn't dare for fear of someone overhearing.

The dance brought them together, and she placed her hand flat against his. How large it was compared to hers.

"You and Jorden looked to be enjoying yourselves."

"Aye, we were."

She couldn't read his expression, wasn't sure if he was jealous or mad. "He asked me to relay a message to Elspeth."

Was that relief she saw in those long-lashed eyes? "I see."

"He is a handsome devil, is he not?"

Adelstan frowned, his jaw clenching.

She tried to keep from smiling but failed. "But not as handsome as ye."

"Witch," he said playfully. "You look beautiful tonight. I like your new gown. It makes your eyes even more vibrant."

His words washed over her like warm honey and her stomach coiled tight, sending an ache straight to her groin. "Thank ye."

He leaned in and whispered, "Meet me tonight."

Her heart missed a beat. "Anywhere."

"Can you get to my room without being seen?"

"Aye."

"If it is too risky, do not come."

Nothing and no one would keep her from taking a chance.

The dance ended far too soon, and though she wanted to dance with him again, she knew to do so would cause suspicion. "Until tonight," she whispered, before walking toward Elspeth and Antony.

Rhiannon pulled her cloak closer to her body. Beneath it she was naked, and her body already felt sensitive. She had brushed out her hair until it crackled, and she paced the room, waiting for the guard to make his usual march up the tower steps.

Elspeth must have met with Jorden, because she had yet to return. Rhiannon could only imagine the two of them now, no doubt making love feverishly, neither one bound by their heartstrings to the other.

If only she could be so casual about sex, her life would be a lot less difficult.

The guard's heavy footfalls approached, and she held her breath, hoping he would not stop, but just keep on going. From time to time her father had placed a guard or two outside her door, but normally that was in way of punishment for having done something wrong.

The footsteps stopped, the person hesitating outside her door before continuing up the steps. She waited long minutes until the footfalls faded.

Heart pounding wildly against her breastbone, she stepped out of her room and headed down the stairs. She rounded the corner to Adelstan's chamber, and had one hand on the door handle when her father appeared.

She gasped. "Father, what are ye doing here?"

"I would ask ye the same question, Daughter, though I fear I already know the answer."

She looked over her shoulder, half expecting Adelstan to open the door and help remedy the situation.

"He is not here. I asked him to watch the east wall for an hour or two since we are shorthanded."

Knowing it would be best to lie, she opened her mouth, but her father's cruel gaze silenced her.

"Ye will be leaving Castle MacKay day after tomorrow. I will see everything is arranged. I am sending a messenger tomorrow morning telling Lord Malgor to expect ye shortly."

Fear clutched her heart. "Father, I am not ready to leave Castle MacKay."

He had never looked so fierce, his eyes narrowing into cruel slits. "Because ye love your home and your people so? Or is it because ye have no wish to meet your betrothed because ye have already given yourself to another?" He shook his head. "Your mother would be so ashamed of ye."

"My mother would understand and sympathize with me."

He lifted her chin with rough hands. "Ye will marry Lord Malgor, Rhiannon. Put this infatuation behind ye, and be a good wife and mother. Ye will do this for your people, Rhiannon. Ye will do this for your mother and I."

SIXTEEN

After a sleepless night, Adelstan rose to a cool September morning. When he had returned to his chamber, he had tossed and turned, knowing exactly why Rhiannon's father had asked him to stand in as watch last night.

Perhaps he and Rhiannon had become too obvious with their affection toward each other. Mayhap during the dance he had read their body language, or noticed how close they had become? Adelstan had hardly helped matters by being unable to take his eyes off her from the moment she'd entered the great hall. He could not help himself. The kirtle had formed to her perfect body, defining the slender lines and supple curves, making him ache for the moment he could take the gown off and feel her beneath him once more.

Walking to the garderobe, he drew out his cock and pissed, wondering if he should stroke himself to find some relief since his balls were full and heavy.

Having emptied his bladder, he stroked his cock from tip to root and back again, while he looked out the small window that allowed for ventilation.

Only servants were up this early, preparing for the day ahead. A chicken rushed across the bailey, the cook chasing after it. The sides of his mouth curved, until he caught sight of a slight figure looking anxiously about as she exited the castle's side entrance.

His heart jolted.

Was it Rhiannon? He pushed his cock back into his braies and watched. It took only seconds to recognize her walk, the small ladylike strides, the erect shoulders, and the way she lifted her chin.

What was she up to?

Good lord, she did not mean to escape, did she? Certainly she would take Elspeth with her if that were the case, or at the very least, some clothing and food.

Intrigued and a bit angered, he tied the cord of his braies, and slipped on his chausses, boots, and tunic, before grabbing his mantle.

By the time he caught up to her, she was walking the familiar road past the village, and toward the marketplace. His mind raced. The market would not be set up yet. Her steps were hurried, and several times she looked back. She appeared anxious.

He intentionally stayed farther behind, in the trees.

How foolish of her to leave the castle alone. Did she not realize the danger in doing so? Any kind of vagabond could come this way and mistake her for a common servant. He knew how often women were raped in such instances, and many times the rapist was never reprimanded. The thought of such an event happening to Rhiannon made his blood run cold.

As the village came into view, he quickened his pace, staying closer now. She walked to a small hut, and once again looked about, before knocking on the door.

Several minutes passed when Gerard, the young goldsmith from the marketplace, answered. He looked shocked to see her, but pleased at the same time.

Adelstan's gut twisted.

What the hell was she up to?

He could not hear them, or even make out what they spoke of. Gerard motioned her inside, and she followed, closing the door behind her.

Not wanting to risk the chance of being caught staring into the window by a neighbor, Adelstan settled in to wait. A rooster crowed, and he heard movement in a nearby hut.

Should he barge in? He was half tempted to do just that when the door opened and Rhiannon appeared with the young man in tow.

They ended up at a shop not far from Gerard's house. The shuttered windows gave him limited visibility into the shop, but Adelstan could see a furnace and tables and tools lying about.

Rhiannon sat on a table, looking completely relaxed as the boy showed her something. She nodded, and Gerard immediately set to work with hammer, anvil, and chisel. As the minutes ticked by, the two talked without end, laughing often and always smiling.

Adelstan had seen the desire in the younger man's eyes at market, and had not been too concerned at the time, and yet now he could not deny the jealousy that coiled within his belly.

Once the boy had finished, Rhiannon looked overjoyed. She threw herself into his arms and Gerard's arms wrapped around her slender body, pulling her close. Her face lay against his chest, and even from here, he could see the huge grin on her face. She looked up at the young man and rested a hand against his jaw. Minutes ticked by endlessly as they talked, nose to nose, and when the boy kissed her forehead, Adelstan nearly made himself known.

Rhiannon took something from a leather bag and pressed it into his palm. He kept shaking his head, obviously not wanting to take the offering.

Shoulders slumping, Gerard gave up, and accepted the gift. Rhiannon left him with a final kiss on his cheek.

He did not want to jump to any conclusions, but why had she been so secretive?

Adelstan followed her until they were out of sight of the village, and then moved ahead of her, staying to the trees. Finally, when she crossed his path, he reached out and grabbed her. Her yelp was cut short by the pressure of his hand.

Pulling her up against him, she tried to kick him, but his free arm tightened around her. "What are you about, Rhiannon?"

"Adelstan?" she said, his name coming out muffled against his palm. "What are ye doing here?"

"Following you."

A blush ran up her cheeks, staining them pink. "I needed to speak to Gerard."

"Aye, I could see that, the question is why?"

She shifted on her feet. "I . . . I wanted to tell Gerard that I will be leaving tomorrow."

His heart missed a beat. "Tomorrow? I have not heard the news."

"My father caught me at your chamber door last night. He knows what we are about, Adelstan, and he told me it is time for

me to go to Almeron and marry Lord Malgor. He has made a bargain with him, and it is my duty to fulfill it."

A bargain.

Just as his sister Aleysia had made a bargain with Renaud
de Wulf thirteen years ago. Now it was Rhiannon who was the
pawn in a bargain.

At least his sister had made the bargain on her own terms.
Rhiannon had not been so fortunate.

Tears swam in her eyes. "I wish I had been born a man."

"I am glad you were not," he said, taking a step closer to her,
but she moved away.

"Do not make fun, Adelstan. I am serious."

"I know. Forgive me."

She ran trembling hands down her face. "Father told me he
would lose too much if this marriage did not take place. If not for
that, I would leave here right now with ye."

Adelstan's stomach churned. "I am sorry, Rhiannon."

"I knew it would be difficult to leave home, but it will be even
harder to pretend I do not care for ye once we reach Almeron."
Tears spilled from her beautiful eyes, down her face, and she
wiped them away with the back of her hands. "I knew this day was
coming, but now that it's here, I feel so helpless."

How beautiful she looked in the morning light. So young, so
innocent, so full of life.

So strong.

And soon she would be another man's bride. The thought
shook him to the core. But this was *his* woman. He did not want
anyone touching her . . . or marrying her.

"Why did you feel the need to tell Gerard good-bye, Rhiannon?"

Her eyes became guarded. "Because he has been a good friend."

"How good a friend?"

She swallowed hard. "I care for him, but not the same way I care for ye."

He pulled her close. His fingers wrapped around her slender upper arms, and she looked up at him, but dropped her gaze almost immediately.

"Then why can't you look at me?"

"At one time I liked Gerard as more than a friend, but all we have ever done is share a kiss. A simple peck on the lips, nothing more."

Even though it was just a kiss, a peck on the lips at that, and before Adelstan had come into her life, he was still jealous.

"Why not send him a letter then to say your good-byes?"

She opened her mouth to speak, then closed it, as her gaze dropped to his chest. "I asked him a favor while at market the other day."

His mind raced. He had left the two alone for only a few minutes. "What favor?"

"Gerard is a goldsmith's apprentice and a good one at that. I asked him to make me a gift for someone. I thought I would pick it up next week on market day, but since we are leaving for Almeron on the morrow, I had to ask him to finish it now. So that is why I was so secretive." She met and held his gaze. "I swear it, Adelstan."

A gust of wind blew, sending a tendril of hair across her lips. He brushed it back, feeling the texture between finger and thumb. His heart ached with the emotion he felt for her. "What is the gift?"

Reaching into the small leather pouch, she pulled out a ring that rested flat on her palm.

He picked it up and recognized immediately a favorite Celtic pattern Aleysia had embroidered on many of his tunics and mantles. It had been his mother's favorite pattern.

His throat grew tight. The ring was for him.

"I guessed at the size. I hope it fits." She slipped the ring onto his finger.

She looked up at him with hopeful eyes. "I know it might seem—"

He kissed her hard, touched by the gift. All the jealousy he had been feeling melted away as her arms slid around his neck. "Thank you, Rhiannon. It's beautiful."

Rhiannon's back came into contact with the giant oak. She felt the hard ridge of Adelstan's cock against her belly, and her passion built quickly, sending white-hot need through her entire being, especially to the flesh between her legs.

Adelstan lifted her skirts and touched her smooth thighs and the heated slit between them. He stroked her, brushing over her clit and around it, before sliding within her blazing core.

"So wet," he said, sounding pleased.

With her need reaching fever pitch, she couldn't stand still and moved against his fingers. As his thumb brushed over her tiny pearl, she cried out as she climaxed.

Adelstan felt her tight muscles squeeze his fingers, her hot essence drenching his fingers.

She touched his cock, her hand molding the material around his rigid length, and he nearly spent himself. Her fingers quickly worked the cord of his braies, and she gripped him hard. He kissed her forehead and closed his eyes as she slid her hand up and down his thick shaft.

His fingers brushed over her clit again, and she drew her hips away. He smiled as she looked up at him, but the grin died the moment he saw the intense need in her eyes.

"I want ye inside me."

Needing no further urging, he lifted her so that her legs wrapped about his waist. Thrusting inside her, he moaned as her slick heat surrounded his cock.

Rhiannon kissed Adelstan as he made love to her, pumping in and out of her with long, fluid strokes. She looked into his eyes and saw the desperation there.

The familiar stirring began, and each thrust brought her closer to orgasm. She looked down, watching as he entered her and withdrew, his cock wet and glistening, the thick veins running along the length, from base to crown.

His fingers dug into her hips as he increased his rhythm, thrusting deeper each time. "Come with me, Rhiannon."

He settled his cock deep within her and cupped his hips, putting friction against her clit, and he was rewarded as her inner muscles clenched him hard, her cries silenced by his mouth. He followed shortly behind, so caught up in the moment he forgot to withdraw and instead came inside her, staying there even after the last quivering of her sex.

Slowly releasing her, she slid to her feet and pulled the skirts down around her while he tied the cord of his braies.

"We had best return before my father finds us both missing."

He stared at her for a long moment. There were so many things he longed to say. So many words left unspoken, and he had no idea if he ever again would get the chance once they returned to

Almeron. After all, even when they left, they would be surrounded by his men, all who could not find out about the relationship, since some men were de Cion's friends as well as Adelstan's.

His father had always told him to hold tight to what he cherished most, and Adelstan could not help feeling as if he was making the biggest mistake of his life by letting Rhiannon marry de Cion. However, what choice did he have? He would marry her in a heartbeat, but he had no land of his own to offer her. He kicked himself, knowing she would be his if only he hadn't bowed out of the running. True, he was next in line for a fief, but the documents had already been signed, the money exchanged between de Cion and Rhiannon's father.

The sun had just risen, casting a glow into the trees, straight down on Rhiannon. His throat went dry. In the early morning light, with her cheeks pink from their lovemaking, her violet eyes glittering, she had never looked so amazing.

"What is it?" she asked, tilting her head the slightest bit.

"Don't move. Stay just like that." Her beauty staggered him, and he knew he would never forget how she looked at this moment.

Rhiannon's stomach tightened as Adelstan continued to stare at her. What scared her more than his intense expression was that it appeared as if he was trying to memorize her features. Was this the end of it then? Would they never again know a moment's peace? Fear and desperation made her want to lunge into his arms.

He blinked a few times, smiled softly, and took her by the hand. She reveled in the feel of their fingers entwined. The moment they hit the tree line, he dropped her hand and looked about.

She glanced at the ring on his long-fingered hand. Should she tell him of the inscription inside the band? Let him know her heart would always belong to him and no other?

Or should she let him find it on his own one day. Perhaps by then, what they had might be nothing but a memory.

SEVENTEEN

"Are you homesick?"

Rhiannon glanced up at Elspeth, who had just roused from a nap. The carriage in which they rode shifted, causing her to reach out and hold on to the window post. They had been traveling for three days now, the bumpy roads making her bones ache.

"A little, and ye?"

Elspeth brought her feet up to rest on the bench. She hugged her knees to her chest and smiled sadly. "I shall miss my grandparents, but they are happy for me, telling me I will have a better life in England." She sighed. "I miss Antony's company, though I was getting a bit tired of his possessive nature. He thought it fair for him to have relations with other women, and yet when I did the same, he called me all kinds of horrible names, so in that, I suppose I am glad to be leaving."

"Ye deserve better than him anyway," Rhiannon said, lifting the fabric from the window. Just as he'd been all morning, Adelstan rode alongside the wagon. His shoulders were straight as the horse galloped along.

As though sensing her presence, Adelstan turned, and Rhiannon let the fabric fall back into place.

"I think he was with Machara the last night at home."

Frowning, Elspeth replied, "Why do ye think that?"

"Did ye see the way they carried on? How I yearned to throw the warm wine in her face when she kept finding reasons to return to the table. I cannot stand that woman."

Elspeth grinned widely. "Ye no longer have to see her again."

"Thank God for that."

"Actually, I believe Adelstan behaved as he did for your father's benefit, and to draw attention away from your relationship."

"Do ye think so?"

Elspeth nodded. "Adelstan cares for ye, Rhiannon. I see it in his eyes when we are away from the others. He longs for ye, and ye for him."

"He has not even looked at me since leaving."

"Only because of his men."

"Does Jorden know about us?"

Elspeth shook her head. "I don't think so."

A knock sounded near the window. "Lady Rhiannon."

Rhiannon's heart jolted. "Adelstan," she whispered, and Elspeth's eyes rounded.

Taking a deep breath, Rhiannon pulled the fabric away and her heart missed a beat as she looked up at him. Deep, dark under-eye circles made his green orbs even more intense.

"Lady Rhiannon, we will travel for an hour and then make camp. It has been a long day, and I'm certain you are both tired."

"Aye, we certainly are. The carriage is beating us half to death."

Concern knitted his brow. "Mayhap tomorrow you can ride, if you are up to it."

"I would like that." She glanced at Elspeth, who nodded. "And Elspeth, too."

"Very well. I shall tell the men to find a safe place to make camp." With a curt nod, he rode off.

"He is so tortured, Rhiannon."

"Tortured?"

"Aye, he feels so deeply for ye, and yet he knows it cannot be. If I could, I would fix this for ye in order to save ye from the pain. I blame myself. I do."

"Ye are not to blame. No one forced me."

Elspeth sighed heavily. "But I encouraged ye."

"If Baron de Cion would have come to Castle MacKay himself, then neither myself nor Adelstan would be in such a dilemma."

"How do ye know ye would not feel the same for Adelstan once ye met him at Almeron? Attraction is attraction."

Rhiannon frowned. "Because I would have never mistaken Adelstan for my betrothed, and I would have gotten to know Lord Malgor by that time."

"But what if ye did not like de Cion's personality, and then ye met Adelstan and the attraction was instantaneous? Would ye still deny yourself the chance of having more with him?"

Rhiannon opened her mouth to respond, but clamped it closed. When she had met Adelstan, her heart had nearly leapt from her chest and the hair on her arms had stood on end. Never had she met anyone so beautiful, or wanted someone so badly. "I would be attracted to him, to be sure, but with de Cion courting me, I would not have the opportunity to spend any time with Adelstan. Therefore, I would not have gotten to meet him the way I have here. I would have had to accept my fate."

Elspeth smiled slowly. "I envy ye in the way ye believe in fate and that there is one man for every woman."

"Do ye not agree?"

She shook her head. "Nay, but I have not been fortunate enough to meet the man who I can envision spending the rest of my life with."

"Perhaps one day ye shall."

"Perhaps," Elspeth said, sounding like she hoped the day would not come too soon. "Meanwhile, I'm having a wonderful time with a certain dark-haired Norman knight."

"Whatever became of his young lover, do ye think?"

"Have ye noticed the light-haired knight in our entourage?"

Rhiannon's eyes widened. "The one with the sandy-blond hair? Aye, he's lovely. Why do ye ask?"

"That is the knight Antony mentioned."

"Are ye certain?"

"I saw him watching Jorden last night when we ate, but dismissed it since Jorden didn't pay him much mind." She shrugged. "I can certainly see the appeal."

Rhiannon laughed under her breath. "I envy ye in your ability not to be jealous, and to look at making love in such a candid way. When it comes to Adelstan, I am jealous of every woman I see talking to him, touching him, even in an innocent way."

Elspeth smiled. "Ye really care for him?"

"Aye, I do. In fact, I do not think I will ever feel about another man the way I feel for Adelstan. There could be no man more beautiful or perfect to me. I would not change one thing about him."

"Dearest Rhiannon, ye amuse me."

"Ye think me a fool?" Rhiannon asked.

Shaking her head, Elspeth replied, "Nay, I think ye are in love."

Adelstan spent the first two hours after making camp chopping wood for the fire. It had been a difficult journey already, but the days ahead would be even more so.

Whenever they stopped to rest, eat, or camp, he could feel Rhiannon watching him, and always he ignored the stare, not wanting anyone to guess at the true nature of their relationship. He also tried to ignore the fire burning within his veins.

God help him but he wanted her. He saw her face in his dreams, and she was the first thing he thought of when he opened his eyes in the morning and the last thing when he closed them each night.

"Sir, the women have asked if I could take them to the river."

"For what purpose?"

Jorden smirked. "I would think to bathe, sir. After all, it has been three days."

"Of course," Adelstan said, feeling foolish. He knew Jorden had started a romantic relationship with Elspeth, and yet he also heard from Jorden's own mouth that he fancied Rhiannon, and thought her beautiful.

"Do I have your permission, sir?"

Adelstan nearly handed him the axe and told him to continue chopping while he took the women to swim, but decided against it. "Aye, you may escort the women, but not too far since supper will be ready soon."

"Very well, sir," Jorden said with a grin. "Are you certain you do not wish to join us? I believe Lady Rhiannon would enjoy your company."

"What makes you say that?" he asked, his voice coarser than intended.

Jorden shrugged. "No reason, besides the fact she is always happiest whenever you are around."

If Jorden had seen as much, did the other men, too? "It stands to reason she feels a kinship with me since she originally mistook me for her betrothed."

Jorden nodded. "She will be most surprised when she meets de Cion in the flesh, and I must say, I do not think it will be a pleasant surprise."

"He is not so old."

"To us, perhaps, but to a young woman of her age, he might appear ancient." He ran a hand through his long, dark hair, his expression turning serious. "My sister's marriage was arranged. She was but five and ten, and her betrothed two and forty. We all knew she loved another, but the boy was of lower station than she, and therefore their love could never be. I was only one year older than she when she came to me asking for my help. I was so fearful of my parents' wrath that I refused. On the eve of her wedding, she escaped into the night, never to be heard from again."

"And her lover?"

"Disappeared as well." Jorden raked his top teeth over his bottom lip. "I think of her every day. I respect her for having the temerity to change her future, even if that future would be harder than being the wife of a wealthy count."

"Indeed, she was very brave." Adelstan shifted on his feet. "If given the chance again, would you help her instead of refuse her?"

"Aye." He snapped his fingers. "That fast."

Not at all surprised by the answer, Adelstan grinned. "Perhaps one day your paths will cross again."

"Perhaps," he said, as though he did not believe it would happen. "Well, I have kept you from your chores for long enough."

"You may help if you'd like."

"Nay, I think not."

"Remember, be back shortly."

"We shall."

Adelstan watched from the corner of his eye as Jorden and the women left camp and made for the river. Everything within him yearned to follow, to spend a few quiet moments with Rhiannon. But to do so would make the final parting all that more difficult.

The majority of the men either rested in their tents or sat around the fire, drinking ale and telling tales, or talking about recent battles. All save Dante, who stood, stretched, and glanced toward the path the three had taken. He walked toward it a moment later.

Jorden wouldn't have asked the young man to follow, would he? To what end?

With a hundred different scenarios running through his mind, Adelstan returned to chopping wood for the fire. Physical exercise always took his mind off his troubles . . . especially when that trouble wore a gown and had violet eyes that haunted him all hours of the day and night.

With a muttered curse, he buried the axe in the stump and followed in the direction the four had gone, all the while telling himself he was a fool.

He heard the sound of water rushing on the rocks, and

expected to find them the moment he walked out of the trees. However, they weren't there.

As he continued to walk along the river's edge, he became more and more irritated. Short of calling out their names, he kept walking and it was a good deal later when finally he heard splashing and laughing.

Elspeth's high-pitched laughter made him smile, even though his irritation with Jorden had soured his already bad mood. A loud splash sounded seconds later, and both women laughed.

He saw the four of them long before they saw him. Jorden's clothes had been thrown haphazardly on the large, flat stones at the water's edge, while the women had neatly laid their gowns on tree branches.

Why had he thought for an instant Jorden would stand by and guard the ladies while they bathed?

Rather, Jorden and Elspeth stood in the water, their arms around each other, while Rhiannon appeared busy scrubbing her long hair, uninterested in what was happening around her.

Dante had just finished stripping, and he grabbed on to a rope fashioned from a tree and dropped into the river, much to the joy of the others. Even Rhiannon smiled before she turned away, rinsed her hair, and proceeded to float on her back, looking up at the sky above her. Adelstan could see she wore her chemise, for all that the transparent material covered. At least she was not naked.

Her arms were out to her sides, her legs splayed a little, and heat rushed straight to his cock, making him hard as marble.

Elspeth and Dante were now splashing each other, and the closer the maid came to the young soldier, the more aggressive she became.

Dante finally held his hands up in mock surrender as she

stood within arm's reach. When Elspeth next splashed him, he laughed and pulled her abruptly to him. His lips claimed hers a second later, and to Adelstan's surprise, the servant did not pull away. Indeed, she seemed intrigued, her mouth opening wide as the younger man kissed her first tentatively, then ravenously.

Jorden stood back watching, his head tilted to the side as though he could not quite believe what he was seeing.

And he was not the only one. Rhiannon, who had just finished rinsing her hair, now watched the two with lifted brows. She dipped her head back in the water, and then standing, brushed her palms over her forehead and scalp, to the back of her head.

If Dante had kissed Rhiannon like that, he would have killed the other man, not stood back and watched with fascination. But Jorden had always had a different way of looking at everything.

Rhiannon looked over at the three a few times, and finally stepped from the water. She might as well have been naked. The chemise clung to her slender form, outlining her perfection. Her small, rose-colored nipples poked against the thin material.

His cock bucked in response.

She took her hair in her hands, pulled the length over one shoulder, and began to squeeze the water from it.

She turned a little toward him, and he could clearly see the triangle of hair between her thighs. He didn't remember taking the steps, but soon he stood at the river's edge, and she looked up at him, her violet eyes wide with shock. Then she smiled and he was lost.

If not for the trio in the water, Adelstan would have taken Rhiannon in his arms, tossed her on the river's bank, and fucked her until the fire in his veins was quenched.

But would the fire ever be quenched?

He feared the answer was no as she swallowed hard and followed his gaze to the trio. Jorden had approached the duo, and though the blond and Elspeth kissed, it didn't last. With a smile, Elspeth turned and began kissing Jorden, but she still had an arm around Dante's shoulders, her fingers weaving through the young man's hair.

Adelstan lifted Rhiannon's kirtle from the branches and motioned for her to go dress, keeping his back to the lovers behind him. She tossed the wet chemise at him and his mouth went dry. He moved a little to his right so he could see her, and almost wished he hadn't. Her back was to him, her heart-shaped buttocks completely bare to his gaze. He did his best to ignore the deep ache in his cock.

EIGHTEEN

Elspeth's heart hammered hard against her chest. She had never before been with two men at the same time, and she didn't know what had possessed her to accept Dante's unexpected kiss, or why it had excited her the way it had.

But the moment his soft lips touched hers, she was lost. Hearing no argument from Jorden, she was coaxed further when the young knight had touched her between her thighs, his fingers brushing over her slit, almost tentatively, as if he wasn't quite sure what to do. Was he an innocent to the ways of a man and a woman? For some reason the thought that she could teach him a thing or two intrigued her.

The cool water felt delicious against her heated body. She felt Jorden approach, and left Dante to kiss him. His cock brushed against her, and she knew his excitement matched hers.

Four hands touched her all over, and she moaned against Jorden's mouth as she came against Dante's fingers. He was almost gentle in the way he touched her, so different from the way Jorden touched her with such intensity and longing.

"Lock your legs around my hips," Jorden said, lifting her, his cock flush against her burning core. He looked over her shoulder at Dante, and the younger man stepped behind her, his chest flush against her back, his hard length brushing her back passage.

When Jorden had touched her there before, inserting a finger or two within her, the sensation had not been at all unpleasant, but rather a mixture of pleasure and pain that had made her wonder what lay ahead.

Apparently she was about to find out.

"Kiss him," she whispered against Jorden's lips.

He pulled away, just enough to look into her eyes. He must have seen in an instant that she wasn't kidding. In fact, she shifted a little, just enough so the two men could kiss. They pressed their lips together, and it was Jorden whose tongue brushed along the younger man's lips, urging, nay—demanding—entry. And Dante did open, moaning as his tongue slid against Jorden's.

Her heart was not about to slow down anytime soon.

And all along she was pressed between their two hard bodies, both their cocks like stone against her belly and ass.

Dante's finger began to move in and out of her back passage, while Jorden's fingers brushed over her clit. She latched on to Jorden's hard cock, her inner muscles clenching. The young knight inserted another finger in her, stretching her, preparing her.

Elspeth's heart rate increased yet again, liquid fire rushing through her veins as an orgasm claimed her. She dropped her head to Jorden's shoulder, moaned low in her throat.

Jorden broke the kiss with Dante and began kissing her neck, while Dante kissed the nape of her neck, her shoulder, biting into it ever so softly.

She had never been so aroused.

With his free hand, Dante teased one of her nipples into a tight bud, pinching and pulling it between finger and thumb. The sensation went straight to her hot sheath, which positively ached with the need to be filled.

Unable to wait, she guided Jorden's thick cock into her weeping passage. As he thrust home, she cried out in ecstasy, not caring if Rhiannon heard. Elspeth wanted only to feel and experience this moment.

Elspeth rode Jorden's cock hard at first, the blood in her veins like liquid fire.

He slowed her pace, his strong hands bracing her hips as he kissed her and whispered to her in French.

Dante's fingers slid within her faster, the sensation of being filled in both places incredible. His hot breath fanned the back of her neck, and she could feel his excitement.

Reaching behind him, she touched his hard cock, her fingers coaxing him to take her.

His fingers slipped from her, and before she could take a breath, the head of his cock eased into her slowly.

She winced at the intrusion, and both men must have felt her stiffen because they both stopped. Dante said something in French she did not understand, and had no idea if he spoke to Jorden or to her.

She looked at Jorden and saw the softness in his eyes, the desire to give her this, not to judge her, but to share this moment with her. They would not hurt her.

Jorden lowered his head and took her nipple into his mouth, laving it, pulling it gently with his teeth, not moving his hips at all.

Dante's tongue ran along the edge of her ear, before dipping inside it, driving her mad with desire. Then he pushed his hips in slowly, pushing past the tight muscle, impaling her with his cock. Her breath left her in a rush as he settled within her, his heart pounding hard against her back.

Jorden kissed her then, and started to move once more. She didn't budge as Dante, too, began to move, their cocks sliding in perfect rhythm within her, brushing against each other with each thrust.

Dante continued to play with her breasts as he spoke heated words in her ear.

Elspeth came immediately and moaned into Jorden's mouth. He smiled against her lips as she fought for breath, all the while her body coming back to life again as the two men moved in and out of her.

She heard their breathing increase, knew they had to be very near climaxing.

And that's when she felt it again, the familiar stirring within her. She rotated her hips and both men moaned, a sound she would never forget for as long as she lived.

Indeed, this moment would burn in her mind for all eternity.

Dante began to move faster and faster and she knew he'd be first to climax. Seconds later she felt his hot seed fill her back passage, yet he didn't withdraw, staying there instead and pressing his hips hard against her. Jorden came along with her, pulling out of her just in time. He dropped his forehead to hers, his silver eyes staring into hers with pure pleasure.

An awkward few moments followed as Dante withdrew from

her, and after a soft kiss to both Elspeth and Jorden, he began to wash himself, a pleased and slightly bewildered smile on his face.

Elspeth's legs were shaky, and she had a hard time making eye contact with either of the men as they both finished bathing and returned to the shore while she washed between her thighs and hoped for the blood to rush back to her legs.

As she watched both men dress, she smiled to herself, wondering and eagerly awaiting what the future had in store.

Rhiannon exited the trees, her wet chemise rolled in a ball.

Adelstan took the garment from her, and grew harder at the thought of her completely naked beneath the gown. She had such a beautiful, flawless body, and he yearned to discover every inch, every hollow with hands and mouth.

If only they had more time together.

If only she were not marrying Malgor de Cion.

At least if Malgor had been an enemy, then Adelstan would have no problem kidnapping her and marrying her himself.

But if he did so now, he would be labeled a traitor to his king and to his fellow officers, and to his liege and brother-in-law.

They walked along in silence, and soon he found himself slowing the pace, not wanting to return to the camp and end their time alone together. She plaited her hair as they walked, her small, ladylike fingers working deftly. Her essence surrounded him and he breathed in deeply of her sweet scent, smiling softly when she looked over at him.

How shy she appeared. Not at all like the outspoken, headstrong girl he had met less than a fortnight ago.

God, had it only been that long?

She glanced at his hand, and knew she looked for the ring. He had taken it off their last night at Castle MacKay, and placed it in a pouch he kept on him at all times. The beautiful piece only reminded him of what he could not have.

She looked away, but not before he saw the hurt in her beautiful violet eyes.

"Rhiannon."

"Ye do not have to say anything, Adelstan. I understand."

"I want to explain."

She shook her head and quickened her pace, but he pulled her back. Seeing the sheen of tears in her remarkable eyes made him feel wretched. For her to give him the ring had taken a lot of courage. He had seen the fear of rejection in her eyes then and now.

"Rhiannon, come, sit down," he said, taking a seat on a large, fallen tree and brushing off the moss beside him. "Please talk to me."

With an exaggerated sigh, she sat beside him.

"I removed the ring because I didn't want to be reminded of the fact you did not belong to me. That you belong to another."

Water from her hair dripped down her throat, making a path between her firm breasts. Without the chemise, her erect nipples strained the fabric of her bodice, and from his height he could see the soft swell of creamy skin. His cock pressed painfully against his braies. "I did not have a choice in this marriage, Adelstan, and well ye know it."

"Aye, I know. Just as I have no choice but to accept the fact you must marry de Cion."

Their gazes caught and held. If only he could tell her what he yearned to. Tell her he thought of her constantly, even in his dreams. He had never been so confused in all his life, and yet, he had never been so happy as he was when they were together. How he envied a man who was able to marry the woman he fell in love with.

"If I could, I would marry ye," she said softly.

He opened his mouth to respond, but closed it just as quickly.

"Does your silence mean ye no longer want me?" she asked, her voice breaking. She lifted her chin a fraction, her brow raised in question as she waited for him to answer.

He could lie and be done with it and they could go back to being what they were before this moment. And yet, as he looked into her eyes, he found his resolve melting.

"I will always want you, Rhiannon. Always. Nothing will ever change that."

"Not even my marriage to another man?" Tears shone in her eyes, and his heart lurched.

"Not even that."

She grabbed his hands, brought them to her lips. "Adelstan, I will go anywhere with ye. I don't care where, just as long as we can be together. Let us leave here, right now if ye wish—"

"King William is the one who arranged this marriage, Rhiannon. He offered Almeron and your hand to my liege to give to any soldier of his choosing, and he chose Malgor. Renaud is my twin's husband, and I his vassal, obligated by duty and honor to do his bidding. Your wedding is one that shall bring peace."

"Aye, William will marry his French officers to English and Scottish women. Peace through breeding," she said, wiping a wayward tear from her eye.

He cursed under his breath, unable to keep the vision of Rhiannon beneath de Cion from his tortured thoughts.

"Damnit, Adelstan! Why can ye not tell your twin's husband that ye wish to marry me instead?"

"Because they will call us traitors."

"Your brother-in-law would call you a traitor?"

"Nay, but the officers I have fought side by side with all these years might."

She flinched as though he'd struck her.

"So ye will say nothing?"

"It is complicated," Adelstan began.

"Sometimes I wish I had never met ye."

Her words shocked him to the core, and he swallowed hard against the sudden tightness in his throat.

She took only one step before he grabbed her wrist and pulled her onto his lap. She fought against him at first, elbowing him in the gut, but he held her firm, locking his arms around her waist, burying his face in her hair. "Rhiannon, please."

"Let me go, Adelstan. What happened between us is over. It was a mistake, and now I must convince my new husband that I am untouched."

He had expected the words, and yet he could not accept them. Could not accept a life without her in it.

She moved a little, enough to look at him. Before she could say a word, he kissed her, claiming her mouth roughly. She didn't respond at first, and instead sat motionless as he continued to kiss her, softly now, while his hand cupped her breast. He plucked at her nipple and she sighed under her breath, but still didn't touch him in any way. Nor did she bother to kiss him back.

Damn her stubborn nature. Nay, damn *his* inability to say no to her. He craved her too much.

He felt her heart race beneath his hand.

She moved her bottom against his thigh. Shifting so she straddled him, Adelstan brought both his hands to her face, cupping it.

He tried kissing her again, and whether she opened her mouth to say something, he would never know because he took the opportunity to slide his tongue in and stroke the velvety sweetness of her mouth.

"I want you, Rhiannon. More than I've ever wanted anyone. Please believe me," he said against her lips. "If I could change this, I would."

She pulled away and looked down at him with narrowed eyes. "Ye only say that because ye want me one last time."

"Don't say that," he said abruptly, surprised at the anger in his voice.

"Why, ye yourself told me we are bound by honor and duty. Why prolong the inevitable?"

"We are bound by honor and duty, but that does not mean we must live without . . ."

Rhiannon's heart skipped a beat. Would he tell her he loved her? She yearned to tell him as much, and yet he had taken off the ring. "Must live without what, Adelstan?"

"Without desire. Without caring for each other. I cannot imagine not being able to touch you," he said, his palm covering a breast, "or kissing you." He kissed her softly, and pulled away to kiss her forehead, her nose, each cheek, and her mouth once more. "I cannot imagine never being able to make love to you again. I would sooner stop breathing."

He lifted her skirts, touching her creamy skin as he pulled the garment up to her waist. She untied his braies and grabbed his cock, her fingers wrapping around him.

He eased her up and slid into her welcoming heat. She gasped as his length filled her to the womb, her eyes darkening as he caressed her bottom, urging her to ride him faster.

She moved slowly up and down, taking him into her molten core, hugging him so tightly, he was tempted to spill his seed already.

But not yet. Nay, he would savor the moment, wait until she found her release.

Her hair had started to dry and curl in soft tendrils, which framed her delicate face. Long, thick lashes cast shadows on her prominent cheekbones, and as her full lips opened and her eyes closed, his heart increased in rhythm. Like her, he had no desire to return to the real world, to return to where they must hide their desire from everyone.

Her eyes opened. None of the innocence remained, but in her stead a vixen who rode him hard. "Ye feel good inside me."

Her words filled and inflamed him. He dropped his head to her breasts, took a nipple into his mouth, and teased it with tongue and teeth.

Her hands clenched at his shoulders as she stopped moving, holding his head still as he teased one breast then the other. He placed a kiss over her heart, which beat frantically against her chest, and he urged her with hands on hips to continue to ride him.

Rhiannon's fingers wove through the hair at the nape of his neck, pulling a little as her thighs clamped tight around his hips. Her breathing increased and soon her warm honey slid over his cock, her inner muscles squeezing him tight.

She opened her eyes and the pleased smile on her lips made him yearn to roar to the skies. Instead, he kissed her hard as he found his own release, shuddering as he came deep inside her.

They stayed like that, his cock still semihard within her hot sheath, her head resting on his shoulder. He kissed her shoulder, her neck.

When would he ever get enough of her?

Never, came the answering reply.

Just as his heart rate started to return to normal, Adelstan heard a twig snap in the distance.

Dread filled him when he looked up and saw Jorden, Elspeth, and Dante in the distance. His friend's face showed shock, as did the younger officer. Elspeth closed her eyes and ran a hand down her face.

"Adelstan, what's wrong?" Rhiannon asked, looking over her shoulder. "Oh my God." She scrambled to her feet, pulling her skirts down around her. "What do we do?"

Standing slowly, Adelstan came to his feet, a heaviness filling his chest as he tied his braies. Jorden and Elspeth he did not worry about, but the younger soldier concerned him, especially since he knew so little about Dante's past. He could very well be loyal to de Cion already, which meant both he and Rhiannon could be in trouble.

"There is nothing we can do now, Rhiannon," he said, taking her hand, bringing it to his lips. "I take full responsibility for my actions."

To his surprise, the concern in her eyes faded, replaced with something that, dare he say it, resembled love.

Jorden could scarcely believe his eyes. He had known Adelstan and Rhiannon had a close relationship, and were good friends, but he had not thought it would ever go beyond a simple flirtation.

Adelstan was too loyal, and his duty meant everything to him, as did his honor.

So what in God's name was he thinking by defiling Lord

Malgor's betrothed? Lord de Wulf would be furious, and true, it would help that Adelstan was their liege's brother-in-law, but that would not save him from the wrath of King William.

And everyone knew King William had called for his head once. He would not hesitate to do so now, de Wulf or no de Wulf.

True, Rhiannon MacKay was a beauty to behold. He himself had lost his breath when he first looked into those violet eyes. No doubt it had been the same for Adelstan, but they had formed a deeper connection.

No wonder his friend had become so quiet of late. So distant.

Dante looked at him, alarmed. Jorden grabbed his hand and said, "You say a word to anyone, and I shall kill you, is that understood?"

Looking shocked by the words, Dante merely nodded.

"Take the women back to camp. We shall be along shortly."

Elspeth, who had been silent since coming up on Rhiannon and Adelstan, nodded and walked toward her charge. To her credit, Rhiannon did not appear embarrassed. Instead, she touched Adelstan's arm and whispered something in his ear before joining Elspeth and Dante.

Adelstan ran a hand through his hair, watching as the three disappeared. Jorden was shocked to see he actually trembled. "Adelstan, what in God's name are you thinking?"

"I can say nothing of my own defense. I wanted her from the moment I met her, and I stopped at nothing to seduce her."

Jorden looked into his friend's light green eyes. "I know you too well, and you would never seduce an innocent. I have seen the way she looks at you and the way you look at her. I just never imagined things had progressed so far. Had I known, I would have made sure Dante did not—"

"Dante is the least of my concerns right now."

"How will she explain her lack of maidenhead come her wedding night?"

Adelstan flinched as though struck, and Jorden could see the torture in his friend's eyes. Rhiannon's impending marriage to their liege had to be torturing him. "There are ways."

"I would take no chances. You know Malgor is a suspicious man anyway. End it now, Adelstan."

Taking a deep breath, Adelstan planted both hands on his hips. "We will just have to be discreet."

"You will continue to see her after we arrive at Almeron?"

"I do not know."

"Adelstan, this is madness. You have managed to carry on an affair without anyone else knowing, but what if de Cion himself finds you in such a position as I found you this evening? You will be killed for treason, and Rhiannon as well. Indeed, I think he would kill you both in a rage before he had the chance to torture either *of you*."

"I would die a happy man at least."

He shook his head. "Tell me this, my friend, will you be happy knowing each night your lover sleeps with another man, perhaps the very same day you do?"

"Shut your mouth, Jorden, before I shut it for you."

Jorden crossed his arms over his chest. "What if she has a child, whose will it be?"

"You might find yourself in a similar position with a certain servant, so I would be careful if I were you."

"*Touché.*"

Adelstan frowned. "My quarrel is not with you, Jorden. I have done this, and I accept all responsibility."

"I wondered about the abrupt departure from Castle MacKay. Did her father know?"

"Yes, he discovered her coming to my room one night."

"No wonder Elspeth was always wanting to be alone with me when the four of us were together."

"You underestimate yourself," Adelstan said with a strained smile. "Elspeth likes you, and her feelings are sincere."

"She knows the truth." It wasn't a question.

Adelstan nodded. "Yes."

Jorden snorted. "Rhiannon's servant knows and yet I am your best friend and I had to find out this way."

"Why bring anyone else into this mess?"

"Break it off while you can, my friend."

Adelstan reached overhead and picked a leaf off a branch, rolling it between his fingers. "You don't understand. It's not that easy."

"What you need is a willing whore in your bed as soon as we return to Almeron. What of de Cion's niece? She was always slipping into your bed at Braemere. Perhaps she can help ease the pain?"

"I don't want anyone else in my bed but Rhiannon."

Jorden ran his hands down his face, frustrated.

"You are my friend, Jorden, and I respect you as a man and as a soldier. If you decide to tell de Cion what you know, I will understand."

Jorden's hands fell to his sides. "Fuck you!"

Adelstan reared back. "What?"

"I swore an oath to defend king and country, and I have always done that. However, I will not betray my best friend and the woman who loves him, not even to King William. If you think me capable of betraying you, then you wound me greatly."

Adelstan stared at Jorden for a long, awkward moment. Relief and something else shone in his eyes, and he took the steps that separated them and embraced him. "Thank you, my friend, for your honesty and your loyalty. I owe you."

Jorden hugged him back, realizing it was the first time they had ever embraced in all the years they had known each other. "And I shall remind you of that at every given opportunity." He put Adelstan at arm's length. "Be careful, Adelstan. Watch yourself. We have both seen Malgor in battle and know what a fierce adversary he can be. He would be merciless if he discovered the truth."

"Then I pray he never does."

NINETEEN

Almeron Castle, The Borderlands

Lord Malgor welcomed Rhiannon to Almeron in grand style.

The carriage approached Almeron Castle, a lovely fortress made of gray stone, surrounded by hundreds, if not thousands, of trees, nestled against a large river . . . just as Adelstan had said.

A legion of people had gathered to greet her, but Rhiannon's gaze settled on a tall, barrel-chested man standing at the head of the pack. He looked a good decade older than her father. "That must be de Cion."

Elspeth squeezed her hand tight. "Aye, I do believe it is."

Unable to say anything else for fear of bursting into tears, Rhiannon took a deep breath to steady her emotions. She must endure what was to come, even if it killed her.

As the carriage finally rolled to a stop, she said a silent prayer before the door opened and Adelstan appeared.

Her heart gave a jolt. How handsome he was, his windswept hair falling to broad shoulders, his light green eyes filled with an anguish she felt all the way to her soul. He looked at her, swallowed hard. "Lady Rhiannon, we have arrived," he said softly. He took her hand, helped her down the carriage steps.

His hand slipped from hers almost immediately, and it took everything she possessed not to grab for it.

Do not leave me, Adelstan.

Just last night they had made love under the stars in the forest not far from Almeron. They would have made the castle last night, but she pretended to be ill, knowing once she arrived at the castle, precious time away would be rare, if not impossible.

"Lady Rhiannon," came a booming voice, laced with a surprisingly thick French accent.

Elspeth stood directly behind her, and she rested a hand on the small of Rhiannon's back, her way of giving small comfort in this most horrible moment.

With firm resolve, Rhiannon looked into the dark brown eyes of her betrothed and forced a smile. To his credit, Malgor de Cion must have been a handsome man in his day, his red hair still thick, though streaked with gray, his eyes framed by dark lashes, his features not too dominating for his face. He was dressed in an expensive tunic of dark green, with thick embroidery at the neck and cuffs, a stunning brooch of gold and emeralds holding his fur-lined mantle together.

"Come, let me see you," he said, walking a wide circle around her, which made the soldiers lined on the walls behind him laugh and applaud. Beside her, Adelstan straightened, the nerve in his jaw clinching.

Malgor wore a cocky smile, inspecting her like one would horseflesh. "Beautiful. Absolutely beautiful. I am well pleased."

Rhiannon bit the inside of her mouth to keep from saying something she would surely regret.

He came full circle to stand in front of her. "Already I yearn for our wedding night."

Only those close by could hear him, Adelstan and Jorden included. She watched them from the corner of her eyes, and neither one laughed.

Malgor must have seen their lack of humor for he looked at the duo, the smile on his mouth thinning. "So somber, Cawdor. And what of you, Louvet?"

"We are both tired, my lord," Jorden said, while Adelstan remained silent. He glanced at Rhiannon, and she wanted to cry for the anguish she saw in his eyes.

Forgive me, those eyes said before he dropped his gaze.

Malgor clapped Adelstan on the back. "Thank you for bringing my bride to me safe and sound. Robert shall show you to your quarters, where you can bathe and relax until this evening when we celebrate and feast."

Adelstan nodded and walked off with Jorden at his side, over the drawbridge and into the bailey. Rhiannon's gaze followed him, noting a lovely woman near her own age calling out his name. He merely nodded in greeting but kept on walking, following Robert into the bailey.

Jealousy ate at Rhiannon's innards, but she pushed the sensation aside.

Malgor took her hand with his beefy, calloused one, and they followed behind the man who had stolen her heart. Villagers and officers alike filled the bailey, leaving only a small path.

Rhiannon could still see Adelstan ahead. The woman had

caught up to him, and now walked with him, her hand winding around his arm.

"Our bedchamber is in this tower." Malgor motioned in the opposite direction Adelstan was walking. "You first, my lady." At the tower steps, Malgor dropped her hand and motioned for her to go before him.

Rhiannon looked to Elspeth and held out her hand. Elspeth's hand tightened around Rhiannon's, and Malgor frowned.

They came to the first door and she hesitated. "Nay, it is the top chamber, my lady."

Feeling Malgor's gaze on her backside the entire way, Rhiannon stopped before the third and final door. He reached beside her and opened the door, his hand brushing against her breast.

He smelled of ale and onions.

"Here is our chamber." He pushed the door open with his foot, and she walked in, more than ready to be away from his disquieting touch.

The stone walls were covered with large tapestries of religious significance, and the large canopy bed with its thick curtains reminded her of her upcoming duty.

Bile rose in her throat.

"I see where your gaze lingers, my lady," he whispered in her ear and she jumped away.

His laughter followed her across the room. The only window was narrow and over halfway up the wall, too far above to reach by chair or bed. Though vast, the chamber had a stifling quality that made her want to run far and fast.

Or mayhap it was just the man beside her who brought about such a reaction.

"Do you like it?"

"Aye." She turned to face him, disquieted to find him right behind her. "But where is my chamber, my lord?"

He frowned, his eyes appearing like slits. "As I already said, this is *our* chamber."

She swallowed hard and forced herself to keep eye contact. "We are not married yet, my lord. It would hardly be appropriate to sleep in the same chamber before the vows have been spoken."

The sides of his mouth curved in a sly smile as his gaze slid down her body, stopping in the vicinity of her breasts before moving downward, over her mons and the girdle's tassels that fell between her legs.

"Nay, we are not married yet, so until that time you will stay in another tower."

Her heart leapt with the hope it was the same tower where private guests and senior officers slept.

"Could ye show me?"

He tilted his head. "Of course."

With hope and excitement running through her veins, she followed Malgor out of the chamber and down the stairs, passing by the two chambers with a sigh of relief.

People still congregated in the bailey, and she forced a smile to her lips, knowing they were excited to greet her and welcome her to her new home.

She had been so stunned upon meeting Malgor, and so fearful that Adelstan had left, she had not taken notice that many had flowers. Making eye contact with an older woman, she smiled and the woman handed her a small bouquet. "Thank ye," Rhiannon said, and one by one, took the flowers offered to her.

She would survive this, and in the end, she would be stronger for it. As they approached the very tower Adelstan had disappeared into, her insides tightened in anticipation. She quickened her steps, leaving Malgor to lag behind, and gasped when she came upon the girl she had seen welcome Adelstan so readily—and Adelstan himself.

He stood in the doorway of the second-floor chamber, his tunic off, but his breeches on. One hand rested on the doorframe, the other on his hip.

The woman had, up to the time Rhiannon had caught them, had her hand on Adelstan's chest, but now she stepped back, nearly running into Rhiannon in her haste. "My lady, I—"

"Forgive me," Rhiannon said, managing to keep her voice even. With a smile she didn't feel, she looked at the girl, and noticed with dread how beautiful she was. She was not dressed as a servant, which led her to believe she was of the noble class.

Malgor caught up to her and glanced at Adelstan, then the girl, exasperation on his face. "Evelyn, it has been a long journey and Adelstan needs his rest. Return to your chamber at once, Niece."

Niece.

Rhiannon's heart dropped to her toes. Did she have a chamber in this tower as well?

Evelyn nodded, and with a passing smile at Adelstan, walked down the steps.

Rhiannon continued up the stairs without sparing Adelstan a glance. Malgor placed his hand on the small of her back, and she felt it like a heavy weight.

She looked back at Malgor when she reached the solar chamber, and he told her to open it, as though she would not have without his permission.

The room was nearly identical to the room she would one day share with him, but instead of religious tapestries, the walls had been washed white. A bouquet of flowers sat on a small table beside the bed.

Thick blankets covered the bed, and a large wooden tub sat before a roaring fire. "I have already asked the servants to fill the bath for you. I am sure after your journey you are ready to relax."

"I am, thank ye," she said, meaning it. She wanted solitude. She needed time to forget about her future and the man who would soon be her husband. "The room is beautiful."

"You like it?"

"Aye, very much, thank ye." She smiled, and he looked relieved. To her chagrin, his dark eyes slid over her again with lust. Did he not realize how unsettling that gaze was, or how rude, particularly in front of others?

"I shall leave you to your bath then. Until tonight," he said, backing toward the door.

She forced a smile until he shut the door, and only then did she allow herself to cry.

Adelstan had never been so miserable.

Sitting to the left of Malgor, he tried without success to keep his gaze from shifting to Rhiannon. But he could not help it. Wearing a beautiful necklace Malgor had commissioned for her, she had never looked more stunning.

He was grateful he had not been asked along on the tour of the chamber she would share with Malgor. In fact, he had been ready to take a bath when Evelyn had knocked on the chamber door. He had hoped it would be Rhiannon, but of course she would be with her betrothed.

When he saw her moments later, coming upon him and Evelyn,

he had been shocked to see her so soon. She had hid her surprise well upon seeing him in an uncompromising position with de Cion's promiscuous niece.

He was surprised Malgor would place Rhiannon in the opposite tower from his own chamber, but had found out from Evelyn the reason. Malgor's leman had claimed the chamber below his, and since Evelyn claimed the first-floor chamber, that left no room for anyone else, including Rhiannon.

All the better for Adelstan and Rhiannon.

Malgor stood, scattering Adelstan's thoughts. "A toast."

Everyone in the hall stood, including Adelstan.

"To my lovely betrothed, Lady Rhiannon, and to the brave knights who fought the wilds of Scotland to bring her to me."

A loud roar of approval filled the hall.

Adelstan tossed back his drink in one long swallow and caught Jorden's gaze. The knight smiled sympathetically before looking at Rhiannon.

He wanted no one's pity. When he had begun the affair, he had known this moment would come. However, he had not imagined feeling so wretched, because he had never imagined falling in love with Rhiannon.

But somewhere along the way he had fallen in love.

His thoughts returned to when they were in Scotland and Rhiannon had been out flying her falcon, flirting mercilessly with the guard in an effort to make him jealous.

Her efforts had worked, for he had been jealous, but that jealousy didn't touch the rage rushing through him now.

Malgor stood and took Rhiannon by the hand, leading her to the floor. "I shall claim the first dance," he said, taking great pride in his duty as lord of the keep.

The music began.

Rhiannon looked like an angel, moving in perfect time to the music, her shoulders erect, chin held high. Malgor watched her with open lust that could be seen by everyone, including his leman, who had just entered by way of the servants' entrance. No doubt he had asked Jocelyn to stay away, but even at Braemere the bold woman had never been one to keep to the shadows. Now she watched Rhiannon and Malgor with an evil smile that didn't begin to reach her eyes.

Two more dances followed before Malgor begged off, and another man took his place. Rhiannon glanced Adelstan's way a few times, but those glances were too fleeting. Did he dare ask her to dance?

Jorden claimed the next dance, and Adelstan could see her relax with his friend, and even smile a few times. All the while Malgor kept an attentive gaze on the two, even as others came up to offer congratulations.

He smiled like a wolf, but then his gaze caught sight of Jocelyn. The smile disappeared instantly.

To her credit, Jocelyn didn't back down from her lover. Indeed, she met him halfway, her hips swaying provocatively. Though she had a decade or more on Rhiannon, she was a beauty, her straight auburn hair falling to her curvaceous waist. Rumor said she had already given birth to three of Malgor's children, but each had been stillborn.

Born a servant, she could not give Malgor what he had wanted so desperately from the time he had taken up arms in King William's army—a fief, a fortune, and a bride of nobility.

But Rhiannon could, and if Adelstan guessed correctly, soon Malgor would be infatuated with his young bride, who would one day give him the son he so craved.

Truth be told, Rhiannon could be pregnant at this very moment with Adelstan's child. The last few times they had made love, he had not withdrawn. Indeed, it seemed she had not wanted him to either, clutching on to him as they came together. Last night he had felt her desperation, and as they lay together in the afterglow, their bodies still joined, he wondered how it would end.

Unable to sit by and watch others dance with her, Adelstan walked toward her.

TWENTY

"May I have this dance, my lady?"

Hearing Adelstan's voice from behind her, Rhiannon breathed a sigh of relief and turned with a smile. Though everyone had been kind thus far, she still felt as if she had few friends here, and it took all her will not to lunge into his arms.

"Of course," she said, nodding demurely, aware of Malgor's searing gaze. The dance was a slow one, and as she took his hand, she squeezed it tight.

I miss ye. I want ye. Take me far, far away from here.

The dance brought them face to face for the space of two counts, and she looked into his eyes.

Meet me tonight.

Though she had only been at Almeron for mere hours, she felt like it had been weeks, if not months, since they had been together, her every move being watched by countless people.

So different from Castle MacKay, where she had had more freedom than she'd realized. Not so here. She would be lady of the keep soon, and life as she'd known it would never be the same. No more stolen moments. Even now Malgor watched her with jealousy in his eyes.

"How are you this evening, Lady Rhiannon?" Adelstan asked, his voice cordial.

Her heart leapt upon hearing her name on his lips. She felt the familiar burning in her veins, the yearning that coiled in her belly, and the wet heat that settled between her thighs. "I am not at all well."

The dance took them away from each other, but soon they were side by side, and his long, warm fingers wrapped around hers. "What do you mean?"

She glanced toward her betrothed to see him talking with an auburn-haired woman. The woman's look was venomous as she turned to stare at Rhiannon. Her angry voice rose above the music, and Malgor took her by the arm and pulled her toward the door. "His lover is not happy I am here."

Adelstan met her gaze. "He will send her away."

"God, I hope he does not."

His gaze searched hers.

"Meet me tonight, Adelstan. Please."

"It is too risky."

"Our chambers are in the same tower, yours right below mine."

The music ended much too soon. Rhiannon bowed and looked up to find her betrothed standing beside Adelstan. The older man grinned widely, his face flushed. "My men must be exhausting you with all the dancing."

"I quite enjoy dancing," she said, irritated by his presence.

"Lady Rhiannon, thank you," Adelstan said with a curt nod, before walking toward Jorden.

Malgor reached out, touched her cheek with his hand in a loving gesture. His hands smelled of venison and onions. She nearly pulled away, but felt all the eyes in the hall watching her, including Adelstan's.

Her cheeks turned hot when Malgor's hand slid to her throat. Horrified, she actually began to tremble.

She felt helpless, alone, desperate.

He lifted the necklace. "Do you like your present?"

"Aye," she said, refusing to meet his gaze. She instead looked at the grease spot on his tunic. Throughout the meal he had slurped his soup and paid little mind that half the contents of the bowl had ended up on him, rather than in his mouth.

His brows furrowed as he lifted the other necklace she always wore, his thumb brushing over the cross.

"'Twas my mother's," she blurted out before he asked the question.

"A nice trinket to be sure, but it cannot compare to the jewels I shall give you." He lifted her chin with coarse fingers, and she was forced to meet his dark, penetrating gaze. "Beautiful jewels for a beautiful woman."

The crowd had hushed to the point one could hear a pin drop. Rhiannon yearned to run away, far from this castle and this man, but instead she stood her ground, letting him grope at her while she ached to spit in his face, and tell him she knew what kind of man he was, no different than her own father, who had abused her mother terribly.

"I cannot wait to marry you. Indeed, I have sent word to my liege, Lord Renaud, asking him to come to Almeron posthaste so that we can be wed immediately."

Her heart sank to her toes. From what Adlestan said, Braemere was but a day or two away from Almeron.

She wanted to tell him no, that she was not ready to wed him, but when she opened her mouth, his fingers squeezed just the slightest bit as though he knew exactly what she yearned to say.

Pressing her lips together, she bit the inside of her mouth and forced herself to meet his gaze.

"By this time next week we will be man and wife." His dark eyes glittered with lust.

"My lord, I am tired and I would very much like to retire to my chamber, with your permission."

Disappointment slid over his features and he dropped her hand abruptly. "Of course, my lady. I shall retire as well."

He cleared his throat loudly. "We shall be retiring. Continue to feast and celebrate the arrival of Lady Rhiannon this night, for in one week she will be my wife."

Roars and loud applause followed the declaration.

Shaking from the top of her head to the soles of her feet, Rhiannon managed to smile when inside she was dying. As she walked toward the door on the arm of her betrothed, she passed by Adelstan and Jorden. They were probably the only two people, aside from herself and Elspeth, who looked disturbed by the news. She caught Adelstan's stare for only a second before looking away. If she wasn't mistaken, he was as miserable as she.

By the time Adelstan reached his chamber, he was more conflicted than ever. His mind told him one thing, while his heart told him yet another.

Pushing the door closed behind him, he reached behind his neck and pulled off his tunic, tossing it aside. He sat down in the chair before the fire, staring into the flames while he worked the laces of his chausses and slipped off his boots.

Running his hands through his hair, he cursed, and stood so fast the chair flew onto its back. How had he made such a mess of both their lives? He reached for the pouch at his waist and took out the ring. He had not worn it since Castle MacKay, and now he looked at it in the firelight.

"Who is it from?" came the soft voice from the bed.

Evelyn sat up on an elbow, allowing the blanket to drop. Her large breasts with rose-colored nipples peeked out at him, and to his surprise, his cock didn't stir.

He placed the ring on his finger. "Evelyn, I am tired."

She looked as though he'd called her a whore. "You must be jesting. You are never one to turn down sex, Adelstan."

He walked to the bed, stood at the edge. "Perhaps, but I am now. I am exhausted."

Her brows furrowed and the blanket slid from her fingers. A heartbeat later she was on her knees before him. She had a pleasing body, and she knew how to use it, but he had already had her too many times and his body craved only one woman.

It was common knowledge Evelyn had been sleeping with the majority of soldiers at Castle Almeron since her arrival. One man in particular, a newly knighted soldier, had already declared his love for her. Unfortunately the girl would use him until she grew tired of him, as was her custom.

Evelyn laid a hand on his chest, her fingers sweeping over his nipple. She leaned in, kissed his neck, her tongue tracing a path up his throat to his chin.

He reached out and grabbed her by the shoulders. "Not tonight, Evelyn. I am tired."

Her arms were around his neck before he could blink, her breasts pressed flush to his chest, and she kissed him.

Behind him he heard the door open, and when he turned, he saw a face in the crack. There one moment, gone the next.

Rhiannon.

His heart pounded hard.

"Who was that?" Evelyn asked, suddenly concerned with her nudity.

"I do not know, but perhaps you should get dressed and return to your chamber before that person returns."

She nodded, and was off the bed and dressing. "Perhaps I can return tomorrow?"

"Your uncle would not take your visits to my chamber lightly, Evelyn."

"We can find other places."

The woman obviously didn't take rejection well. Having lost his patience, he walked her to the door and showed her out.

Rhiannon felt ill.

She still could not believe what she had seen. Thank goodness Elspeth had been there to pull her away from the door, and safely back to her chamber before being discovered by Adelstan and his whore.

She'd had a horrible feeling about that woman from the second she'd seen her welcoming Adelstan. The two had been lovers, and would continue to be . . . and nothing would change that.

"Sit down and I shall brush your hair," Elspeth urged.

"Nay," Rhiannon said, walking toward the side table and the warm wine there. She lifted the goblet to her lips and took a few swallows.

"Perhaps she went there of her own accord. After all, he still had his braies on."

"He was half naked, Elspeth." Her voice broke and she took another drink.

"I am sorry, my dear," Elspeth said, kissing her cheek.

Rhiannon nodded, her mind racing. "We must leave here."

Elspeth went completely still. "Rhiannon . . ."

Rhiannon's heart clenched. "Ye would not leave with me?"

"Remember what your father said to ye? He is bound by this agreement, as are you, Rhiannon."

"Then I shall leave alone."

"Do not be foolish. How will ye survive?"

"I shall find a way."

"Ye are not used to a life of hardship."

Rhiannon shrugged. "I would prefer a life of hardship rather than marry a man I despise, or watch the man I do love flaunt his lover before me."

"Love?"

"Aye, I love Adelstan."

Elspeth closed her eyes and took a deep breath. "If ye wish to leave, I shall go with ye."

Hope filled Rhiannon for the first time in days. She hugged her friend tight. "Thank ye."

Elspeth started to pace the chamber. "In the coming days we

must prepare for our journey. Your every move is being watched, so I shall find the food we will need. Perhaps Adelstan can help?"

"Nay, he must not know. I will not put him in jeopardy, and swear to me ye will not tell Jorden."

Nodding, Elspeth sat down in the nearest chair. "I swear. But how will we escape if Malgor is always watching?"

"I shall find a way."

Elspeth folded her hands together. "Perhaps in time being the Lady of Almeron would not be so horrible."

"I find my betrothed repulsive and he has a leman. When we marry, what makes you think he will not bring her to our bed, Elspeth? I have seen the way he looks at me. I do not put anything past him, even sharing me with his lover is not beyond him. I watched the same happen to my mother, and she was soon cast aside. The difference between us is that I do not love Malgor, nor would I ever."

Elspeth frowned. "Perhaps ye *should* consider telling Jorden at the very least."

"Do ye wish to stay because ye want Jorden?" The words almost sounded accusatory.

Elspeth's gaze fell between them, her cheeks crimson. Rhiannon had often wondered about what happened between her and the two men at the loch that day.

"I will not lie . . . I am enjoying myself."

Rhiannon sat on the floor beside her maid and rested her head against her knee. "I wish I could be like ye, Elspeth. How easy it would be to make love to whomever ye chose, and not let your emotions become involved."

Elspeth brushed her fingers through Rhiannon's hair. "It is not that I don't care for the men I become involved with. I fell in love once, and he crushed my heart. I do not wish anyone to experience such pain, especially ye."

Rhiannon looked up at her, shocked she had not told her so before.

"I was only five and ten, and he twenty. He wasn't very attractive, but I liked his smile. At the time I was a lowly maid in your father's keep, and he worked in the kitchens as the cook's apprentice. He flirted with me constantly, and at first I had no interest, but as the weeks went by, he became more and more handsome to me. One day, he pulled me into the pantry and kissed me."

Elspeth's lips curved into a soft smile. "I could barely sleep that night for all the excitement I felt. For weeks we carried on like that, stolen kisses, and then he grew bolder, touching my breast, squeezing my buttocks. He told me he wanted to marry me, and being young and innocent, I believed him. So after much convincing, he took me to his home in the village. That night he made love to me, and every night thereafter for at least three months. I was desperately in love, so much that when our nights together became fewer, I didn't notice his attention had turned to another servant."

"Oh, Elspeth," Rhiannon said, her throat tightening, reminding her of how she felt seeing Adelstan with Evelyn.

"At the time I didn't understand, and worse still, I found out I was with child. The healer confirmed it, and when I went to his house to tell him the news, I found him in bed with the servant."

"What did ye do?"

"I screamed at both of them, and I remember him scrambling from the bed, and the girl just lay in the bed gloating at me as the man I loved told me he was marrying her." Elspeth closed her eyes, took a deep breath before opening them again. "I went to the healer, and I told her to mix a concoction that would make me lose the child."

"Elspeth . . ."

Elspeth took Rhiannon's face between her hands. "I tell ye this because I want ye to know that even though your heart might be breaking, there is a tomorrow and ye shall love again."

TWENTY-ONE

Elspeth lay naked, flat on her belly on the blanket she had brought with her, in the only room in a weathered old hut outside the village of Castle Almeron. She had taken a chance by coming here, but she needed to see Jorden before she left. Needed to let him know she would never forget him for as long as she lived.

She heard a horse's hooves, and taking a calming breath, she watched the door expectantly.

The door opened suddenly, and Jorden appeared, looking as handsome as ever. "Elspeth," he said, a smile playing at the corners of his mouth as he shut the door with his foot and walked toward her, untying his braies.

He was out of his clothes before she could blink, his powerful body glorious in all its splendor.

Her thighs tightened as his gaze slid down her backside and he grabbed his cock, caressing himself from root to fat crown and back again.

She guessed he might scare many of his lovers, but he didn't scare her. She reveled in his openness, his eagerness to please, his intense sexuality that might make a meeker woman run.

But not her. He excited her in ways no other lover had.

They had not spoken of Dante since the three of them had made love in the river. The younger officer always beamed whenever she walked by or stopped to talk to him, and she had a feeling Jorden had warned him to say nothing to anyone. Once she had noticed Jorden watching the two of them closely, and to her surprise, she had thought she saw jealousy in his eyes.

Whether that jealousy had been directed at her or Dante, she had no idea. It didn't matter. He had given her some much-needed confidence, and she would be forever grateful to him for that.

"Do what ye will with me," she said, sounding less nervous than she felt.

He flashed a devilish grin that made her heart beat in triple time. "That is quite an invitation."

He started kissing her toes, and worked his way up to her ankles, her calves, the backs of her knees, to her thighs.

He spread her legs apart, pulled her hips up and kissed the dimples above her buttocks, before licking her slit from one end to the other.

Her fingers fisted the bedding beneath her.

"Jorden," she said on a ragged whisper and he laughed under his breath, a wicked sound that thrilled her.

He flicked his tongue over her throbbing clit, and over her back passage. Her insides clenched with the need to have him fill her.

His fingers followed his tongue, probing inside her slick heat, while his thumb eased into her ass. He pressed past the tight ring of muscle, and let out a groan. "Mmm, so tight."

"Ye want me there, don't ye?"

His silver eyes turned a darker shade. "Aye, I do."

"But you are soaking wet here," he said, moving his fingers against her sweet spot inside her vagina.

She came against his fingers, enjoying the rippling of his chest as he groaned against her back.

He removed his fingers and thrust his cock inside her, her weeping walls gripping him tight. She arched her back, taking him fully, loving the feel of his heavy sac slapping against her folds.

Taking a handful of both breasts, he played with them, teasing her nipples into tiny little buds, the sensation sending a pulsing pleasure throughout her, centering at where he filled her.

She looked back at him, saw the intensity in his wolflike eyes. He flicked her clit again and again and she came hard, her inner muscles squeezing his thick length tight.

When the last tremors had faded, he pulled out of her, his heavily veined cock still hard and slick.

Her stomach clenched when he placed the head at her back passage and slipped past the band of muscle. "Bear down," he whispered, and she did, biting her lip against the pain. He was so much larger than Dante and she wasn't sure if she could take him.

With a single thrust, he buried himself balls-deep and she cried out at the mixture of pleasure-pain that rippled through her.

Trembling and staying completely still, he bent over her, kissing the nape of her neck, whispering French love words in her ear.

She began to relax, and only then did he begin to move. Instantly her body came back to life, and he knew exactly where to touch her, a hand on her breast, the other at her sex, rubbing her clit and sliding into her heat with expert skill.

The familiar stirring began deep in her belly, and soon she was reaching for the stars, and crying out his name. He followed right behind her, moaning as he filled her with his cream.

Rhiannon tried to keep up with de Cion's long strides. Renaud de Wulf and his bride, Adelstan's sister, had arrived at Almeron, which meant she was days from her wedding.

She felt sick and had been for the past two days. The very sight of food made her stomach churn, and even when she was certain there was nothing left to purge, she continued to heave. Scents were the worst, particularly de Cion's strange odor, which had been one reason she stayed in her chamber.

This morning, when she had thrown up yet again, Elspeth had rung her hands nervously, pacing the chamber, until she finally turned and asked Rhiannon if she was with child.

Rhiannon's menses should have arrived by now, and they had always been timely, which meant she could very well be pregnant with Adelstan's child. Fear and a mixture of excitement filled her at the thought.

"The least you can do is look happy, my dear," de Cion said with a forced smile.

"Aye, my lord." She forced a grin, and he nodded with satisfaction.

Malgor had dressed in his finery, the yellow tunic stretching over his barrel chest. Rhiannon and Elspeth had been up on the ramparts earlier this morning, talking about which direction would be the safest to take upon fleeing. From their position, hidden behind the battlements, she had seen de Cion with his mistress, embracing and kissing before he left the armory. He had patted the woman's behind, while she in turn tossed back her head and blew him a kiss.

Rhiannon could not wait to escape the man, and the hell her life would be married to him.

Hopefully by this time tomorrow she would be long gone from Castle Almeron. She had no intention of returning to Scotland or her father's keep. Instead, she would flee to Wales, near the English border, to a small town her mother spoke about often. No one would ever think to look for her there.

Glancing behind her, Rhiannon looked at Elspeth, who smiled encouragingly, before glancing at Malgor, who cast both of them an irritated look.

It was obvious he didn't like Elspeth, and for no other reason than Rhiannon was close to her. Perhaps he had wanted her to come to Almeron alone and make her own friends? Or perhaps he did not approve of such a friendship between a lady and her servant?

Well, de Cion could go hang for all she cared.

"Here they are," de Cion said, smoothing his tunic as they passed under the gatehouse.

Renaud de Wulf was a tall and imposing figure. He dismounted from a large horse, and reached up to help his wife down. The slender woman beamed up at her husband with true affection.

She knew that Aleysia and Adelstan were twins, and therefore she would be pretty, but Rhiannon was unprepared for the woman's stunning beauty. When she smiled, Rhiannon saw Adelstan and a lump formed in her throat.

"Welcome to Castle Almeron, my lord," Malgor said with a flamboyant bow. He looked to Aleysia and gave a curt nod. "My lady."

Renaud and Aleysia nodded. "Thank you, Lord Malgor. 'Tis a beautiful keep. I did not realize the forest here was so dense. I imagine the hunting is exceptional?"

"Aye, it is. If you wish, we can hunt in the morning."

"I would like that very much."

Renaud's silver gaze settled on Rhiannon and she smiled, her heart accelerating as he grinned. What a gorgeous man, albeit a bit intimidating with the scar running along his right cheek, and other knicks on his powerful forearms and chest. This man was a warrior through and through, and had no doubt seen a lot of war in his time.

"Lord Renaud, may I present Lady Rhiannon MacKay."

Renaud nodded. "It is a pleasure to finally meet you, Lady Rhiannon. I trust your journey from your homeland was not too taxing."

She relaxed, finding his easy nature infectious. "Your men took excellent care of me, my lord, particularly Sir Adelstan."

Aleysia beamed.

"This is my beautiful wife, Lady de Wulf of Braemere."

"And Adelstan's sister," Aleysia was quick to add, obviously proud of her brother.

"Aye, I thought as much," Rhiannon said, her grin matching the woman's.

"Speaking of Adelstan, where is my brother-in-law? Off hunting these woods, I imagine," Renaud said, looking about anxiously.

"Here he comes, my lord." A tower guard above them pointed to the hill.

A moment later Adelstan crested the hill, along with Jorden, both men holding bows. Renaud's laughter rumbled in his chest seeing he had been right.

The two men, who had been talking among themselves, looked up, obviously shocked to find they had an audience.

"Adelstan," Aleysia said under her breath, an enormous smile on her face.

"Go and greet your brother, my dear," Renaud said, love shining in his eyes. "One would think it had been years since she has last seen him."

Aleysia rushed to greet Adelstan, who took her up in his arms and held her tight.

Rhiannon swallowed past the lump in her throat, just as a warm hand squeezed hers. Elspeth.

Two young men and two young girls lunged from the carriage and rushed toward Adelstan and their mother. Adelstan laughed as he hugged each of the boys, and then lifted the girls as though they were as light as feathers.

Rhiannon's heart swelled with love for him.

"They love their uncle," Renaud said unnecessarily. "I told Adelstan he must have children of his own one day, for he will be a fine father."

Reminded of the possibility that she might be carrying Adelstan's child, Rhiannon nodded. "Indeed."

Renaud crossed his arms over his chest. "I hope that watching your wedding will only entice him to take a bride of his own."

Rhiannon's stomach churned and Malgor nodded. "Perhaps."

Adelstan greeted his brother-in-law with a warm hug and finally looked at Rhiannon. He looked exhausted, his face paler than usual, dark circles beneath his light eyes. Lord help her but she loved him. Desperately.

She could feel Aleysia watching the two of them, and Rhiannon dropped her gaze immediately and shifted on her feet. She wanted what his sister and Renaud de Wulf had. Nay—*ached* for what they had.

But she would never know what could be, because she had to leave, for her own sanity.

"Come, let me show you Almeron Castle," Malgor said, leading the group over the bridge and into the bailey.

While de Cion took on the role as lord and master with relish, Rhiannon fell back, hoping to have a moment with Adelstan while Malgor's attention was elsewhere.

Every once in a while she would see Aleysia, who was holding her husband's hand, glance back at her and smile before looking to her brother.

Was it possible she knew they were lovers?

Rhiannon stayed back as de Cion climbed the stairs with Renaud and his family. Adelstan hung back, too, just to her left, so close they nearly touched. "I must speak to you," he whispered.

Her heart missed a beat. She met his gaze, and almost wished she hadn't. The desperation in his eyes made her yearn to give him anything. "There is nothing to say, Adelstan."

"Oh, but there is."

She looked down at his hand and noticed the ring on his finger. The ring she had given him.

"What wonderful craftsmanship. May I see it?" Aleysia asked, surprising them both.

Rhiannon bit the inside of her cheek to keep from saying anything. She had thought Aleysia had gone with her family.

Adelstan held out his hand, but his sister frowned. "Mother's favorite pattern. It's lovely. Was it made here?"

"Nay, in Scotland."

"You were not there all that long."

"You know how melancholy I become while visiting the Highlands."

She smiled up at him. "What a lovely sentiment."

Adelstan frowned. "What do you mean?"

Aleysia stopped in midstep, brows furrowed. "The inscription within, of course."

Rhiannon felt the blood leave her face when Malgor appeared, looking irritated she had not followed their guests. Elspeth looped her arm through hers, but she could not bring herself to look at her friend. The ring had been her secret.

Not anymore.

Adelstan snatched the ring from his sister's hand. She could not see if he read the inscription before slipping it back on his finger, but she saw the nerve dancing in his jaw.

Aleysia walked outside Castle Almeron, watching her twin brother beneath lowered lids. He had been quiet since she had asked to see his ring.

"The R stands for Rhiannon, doesn't it?"

Adelstan nodded, twisting the ring on his finger.

"Brother, what have you done?"

He ran both hands down his face. "I tried so hard to keep it from happening, but I could not help it. She is so beautiful."

"Aye, she is . . . but she is also promised to another."

"You were promised to another."

She lifted a brow, but refrained from saying anything.

"Forgive me. I meant no disrespect, Aleysia."

"I know, Adelstan. I could tell when she looked at you that her feelings went beyond friendship. I just never guessed how far."

"Neither of us planned to fall in love."

"How could you? Love is love, Adelstan. Look at Renaud and I. My God, we were bitter enemies and still we fell desperately in love."

"Renaud sent me to Scotland in good faith, expecting me to bring Rhiannon back to Almeron untouched and chaste. What do I do, but fall in love with another man's betrothed."

"You truly love her?"

Adelstan looked at her for a long, hard moment. "Aye, I do." He cursed beneath his breath. "I know what you must think."

She grabbed his hands. "Nay, you do not know what I am thinking. Adelstan, I do not judge you. I would never judge you, nor anyone else, but especially you."

"I never thought anything like this would ever happen to me. I never dreamed when I arrived in Scotland I would find a young woman who filled me with such exhilaration that I could barely sleep. She haunts my dreams, my every waking hour. I am in hell."

Her lips curved into a soft, knowing smile.

"You think this funny?"

"Nay, I think you are desperately in love and you cannot see a way out."

"I could leave and try to forget her, return to Braemere and go on with my life . . . and yet I cannot bring myself to do so."

"She is beautiful. Those eyes."

He grinned boyishly. "They are incredible, aren't they?"

"Very. And from what I hear, she is quite spirited."

Adelstan laughed under his breath. "Aye, more than you can imagine."

The smile vanished, though, and she could see pain in his eyes. "What do I do, Aleysia? She is to marry de Cion in a few days' time, and it will be too late."

"Let me speak to Renaud."

"He will be furious."

She frowned. "You would rather she marry another?"

He shook his head. "Nay, but I will be ruined, as will she."

"Nay, you will not be ruined. We shall find another bride for Baron de Cion. These lands were given to Malgor by Renaud and have nothing to do with Rhiannon."

"But the dowry."

"Do not worry about the dowry, Adelstan. Let me speak to my husband. Renaud loves you, and he will help fix this. Plus, he likes Rhiannon. He says she reminds him of me."

Adelstan laughed. "And you never did like Malgor, did you?"

"I find him coarse, and I do not care for a man who would parade his leman before his betrothed. Rhiannon deserves better. In fact, she deserves you."

"My men—"

"Adore you, and will follow you back to Braemere, where you will continue to lead Renaud's army until your fief is ready. That day is coming, Brother."

She watched her twin, knew the inner battle playing within his head. "You have been a loyal and true vassal, Adelstan. Always you have lived by honor and duty. You declined promotions you rightly deserved, all because you didn't want others to think you were given them out of preference, because you were family to

Renaud. You should have received Almeron before de Cion and every man here knows that. You are a better soldier than he, and a better man, too."

Adelstan looked up, caught her gaze. "Thank you, Aleysia."

"You are worth so much more than you know." She went up on her toes and cupped his face with her hands. "You have earned the right to have your own lands and titles, Adelstan. Indeed, it is long past due. Your men are so loyal to you, and they would come from every demesne to join your forces if need be. Indeed, Renaud would have to offer them much to stay at Braemere."

He shook his head. "It is just so difficult."

She lifted his chin with her fingers. " 'Love of my heart.' Rhiannon had those words carved in that ring because she meant them, Adelstan. She loves you, and sometimes love only comes around once in a lifetime. You must seize it or watch it pass by. Do you want to look back on your life one day, and wonder what would have happened if you would have just listened to your heart instead of your head?"

He took off the ring, ran a finger over the inscription.

"Sometimes love comes at a price, and sometimes you must choose between love and duty, Adelstan."

TWENTY-TWO

The feasting went well on into the night. By the time Rhiannon made her way to her room, she was exhausted and feeling sick yet again. She had drunk neither wine nor ale, so that could not be the culprit.

"Would ye like a hot bath?" Elspeth asked, concern knitting her brow.

"Nay, I need to sleep. I do not feel at all well."

"Jorden has asked to meet me."

Rhiannon smiled. "And are ye going to meet him?"

"I'd like to . . . unless ye have need of me."

"Go, I can handle Jocelyn."

"Jorden can wait awhile longer," Elspeth said, chewing her lip. "I do not trust that woman very much."

Knowing they had to be certain that de Cion would sleep the night away when they did decide to flee Almeron, Elspeth had told Jocelyn to meet with them after dinner. Hopefully the woman would show soon.

"Nay, I can handle her. Go, enjoy yourself."

"Are ye sure?"

"Aye, now go."

Elspeth kissed her cheek and rushed across the bailey toward the armory.

Rhiannon waited awhile longer, growing impatient by the minute. She was ready to retire when Malgor's leman appeared from the shadows, nearly startling Rhiannon out of her skin.

"My lady," she said with a curt nod.

"Good evening."

"Your maid said ye wished to speak to me." The woman's gaze shifted over Rhiannon in a way that made her uneasy.

Rhiannon forced a smile. "Aye, I was hoping ye could be so kind as to bring Lord Malgor some warm wine this evening."

Jocelyn's eyes narrowed.

"Does the baron not drink wine?"

The leman looked at Rhiannon as though she were daft. "Aye, he drinks wine."

Rhiannon lifted her chin a fraction and squared her shoulders. "His lordship looked extremely tired today, and I know how taxing having guests can be. Since I am not feeling well, I had hoped ye could take care of him this evening . . . tomorrow night as well. Just see that he has wine, mayhap prepare a bath. If ye could do this for me, I would forever be in your debt."

The woman's lips quirked and she bowed her head. "I would be delighted to help in any way, Lady Rhiannon."

"Excellent. Ye are as loyal as they come." Rhiannon kissed her cheek, and the scent of roses met her. She recognized the same scent on de Cion's shirt earlier, mingled with his odd scent.

"Is that all, Lady Rhiannon?" she asked, her gaze once again shifting over her.

"Aye, that is all."

With a nod, Jocelyn rushed off in the direction of the kitchen.

Rhiannon smiled inwardly and started for her chamber. If all went well, then by this time tomorrow she and Elspeth would be well on their way to Wales.

Walking up the tower stairs, Rhiannon thought back on the night. She had watched Adelstan and his sister talking. From time to time she would feel his gaze on her, but Rhiannon would always look away. She could not change her mind about leaving.

Besides, it was obvious Adelstan had chosen duty and honor over her.

She entered her chamber and locked the door, not wanting de Cion to let himself in as he had done on several other occasions.

God willing, his leman would keep him busy all night.

Loosening the laces at her back, she walked toward the hearth. She had been unable to eat much of anything tonight, her nerves stealing her appetite.

Elspeth had mentioned that Rhiannon must eat if she were pregnant with Adelstan's child.

Her hands moved to her flat stomach as she remembered him playing with his nieces and nephews, the look of love and admiration on each of their young faces as he welcomed them.

She had watched Renaud and Aleysia throughout the night, always holding hands, touching each other, their love and devotion obvious to everyone.

Lucky woman.

Lucky man.

A knock sounded at the door and Rhiannon frowned. It was too early for Elspeth to return . . . unless he could not find Jorden. She doubted Jocelyn would come to her room for any reason.

She walked to the door and lifted the latch.

Her pulse skittered. "Adelstan, what—"

He pulled her into his arms and kicked the door closed behind him. His hands framed her face as he kissed her hard, his lips demanding a response.

Her heart pounded nearly out of her chest. She opened her mouth to ask him if he'd lost his mind, but his tongue swooped in, velvety soft, sliding over hers.

His hands were everywhere at once, weaving through her hair one minute, another cupping a breast, sliding down her stomach, touching her damp folds.

He pulled away long enough to lift the kirtle from her body, and yanked the cord of his braies. Pushing the breeches down his hips and kicking them out of the way, he lifted her into his strong arms and kissed her as he walked them toward the bed, and laid her down gently.

Her back had just met the blankets when his cockhead brushed her wet slit.

She touched his chest, his hard abdomen, taking her fill of him, wanting to memorize every detail of his powerful body.

He thrust within her and she cried out his name on a moan. His strokes were long and even, his fingers clenching her buttocks, pulling her closer.

He brushed her clit with two fingers, drawing circles around the sensitive pearl before pressing against it with the perfect pressure.

"Yes," she said, her body climbing toward orgasm. The bed slammed against the wall, matching the rhythm of their bodies, over and over, and anyone walking by could have heard.

But she wouldn't stop him.

He cupped her breast, played with a nipple, rolling it with deft fingers, blowing on the sensitive bud.

Warmth flooded her groin, seeping to her soaking wet women's flesh as his strokes increased, sending delicious shivers through her.

Her orgasm came with a ferocity that shocked her, and she cried out his name on a sob as he kissed her neck, reigniting her passion all over again.

Adelstan kept his climax at bay. He had no desire to come immediately, not when he had been aching to take her for days now. Her violet eyes were dark, her cheeks flushed as she looked into his eyes.

Always having sex had been about the act, never about emotion. He felt her need, her desire, for it matched his own. "I love you, Rhiannon."

Her gaze searched his and tears came to her eyes. "I love ye, too."

His heart soared to the heavens.

She clung to him, her heart pounding against him as they came together.

Adelstan laced his fingers with hers. She brought their hands to her face, kissed the top of his hand, near the ring she'd had made for him.

"Thank ye for wearing the ring."

He rolled off her, bringing her with him, so they lay side by side, face to face. "Thank you for the inscription."

"Ye had not seen it before your sister noticed?"

"Nay, I hadn't."

She reached up, brushing her fingers over his lips. He pursed his lips, kissing the tips.

"I could get used to this," she said with a smile.

"As could I."

She dropped her gaze for a moment, the smile disappearing from her beautiful face.

He lifted her chin. "Do not marry de Cion."

Her heart leapt at the request. "I'm not going to."

His brows drew together.

"Elspeth and I are going to leave tomorrow night."

He went up on his elbow. "When were you going to tell me?"

"I wasn't." Rhiannon sat up, and noticed Adelstan's hungry gaze on her body. "Ye cannot blame me for doing so, Adelstan."

"I spoke to my sister today and she is going to talk to Renaud. I have no idea what he will decide, but I do know this, I am prepared to do whatever I must in order to win your hand."

Malgor cuddled closer to his leman, pleasantly sated. No other woman could suck him off the way Jocelyn could. Indeed, she made him feel more of a man than he was, and he would miss such moments with her. However, his young betrothed was a beauty, far more striking than rumor told, and he ached to take her virginity on their wedding night, which couldn't come soon enough.

"What are you thinking?" Jocelyn asked, her eyes full of concern.

"Nothing."

She lifted a brow, her gaze shifting to the blankets where his small cock bucked. "Your dick says differently."

He knew better than to mention Rhiannon's name around Jocelyn. His betrothed was a sore subject. Obviously Rhiannon had no idea of her station in his life. Why else would she ask her to bring him wine? The two of them had laughed about it. Perhaps his betrothed's ignorance was a good thing. "You feel so good, I cannot help but be eager to take you again."

Her eyes lit up as her hand fisted him.

A knock sounded at the door, and Malgor looked at Jocelyn, wondering if she had a surprise in store for him, as was sometimes her custom. "Are you expecting someone?"

"Nay, are you?"

"Hide yourself," he said, not wanting any of his men to see his whore in his bed, especially Renaud de Wulf. He doubted his liege would come to his chamber at night, especially when he'd been unable to keep his hands off his wife all evening.

Pulling on his braies and tunic, he walked over to the door and opened it to find his niece. "Evelyn, what on earth?"

"Uncle, I must speak with you."

"Can it not wait until morning?"

"Nay, it cannot."

He pulled her inside the door, glancing over at the bed to see the bed curtain had been closed just enough that Evelyn could not see Jocelyn.

"There is something you must know about Lady Rhiannon."

Misgivings rushed up his spine. "Out with it, girl!"

Evelyn pressed her lips together. "Rhiannon and Adelstan are in love. I believe they are together as we speak."

He watched her closely, and then laughed. "You are wrong. Adelstan would never betray me, or his liege. Especially his liege. He takes his duty most seriously."

Evelyn shifted on her feet. "Uncle, you have been deceived. I watched Adelstan go to Rhiannon's chamber this evening. I followed him there, and when she answered the door, he kissed her. I stayed there, listening, and I am certain they made love."

Malgor could have sworn he heard a pleased sound come from the direction of the bed, but if his niece heard, she gave no indication. His mind raced as a murderous rage rushed through him. He thought back on Rhiannon's reaction the day she had come to Almeron, the way her gaze had lingered on the handsome young knight.

If only he had gone to Scotland instead, but nay, he had stayed behind for Jocelyn's sake, telling all others he had wounded himself during a hunt. Aye, he had received wounds all right . . . from Jocelyn's long nails the very night he told her she would not be coming to Almeron with him. She had calmed his temper, though, with her soft words and softer body, touching him in all the ways he liked, pumping up his pride until he convinced himself he could not live without her. He'd stayed in England to prove his devotion to her, while supposedly nursing a wound that did not exist.

Evelyn's eyes widened. "That Scottish whore has bewitched him, I know it."

"Do not call my bride a whore, especially when you yourself have slept with half the men at Almeron already."

She flinched as though he'd struck her. "If you do not believe me, then go to her room now, Uncle. See for yourself the little whore who will be your wife. She has made a fool of you."

His hands clenched into fists at his side. "Perhaps I shall."

Relief shone in her eyes before she left the chamber, closing the door behind her.

As expected, the bed curtain ripped open. Jocelyn sat upon her knees, watching him with a malicious expression on her face. "No wonder she sent me to you. She expected her lover."

"Shut your mouth."

The smile faded. "Why would you marry a woman who has betrayed you so openly, Malgor? Have you no pride?"

"I am beholden to her father."

She made a sound of disgust. "You are beholden to no man. You wish to marry her, even though she fucks another."

"Be quiet, woman!"

"You do not deny it?"

He would not explain himself to a whore. "Leave my chamber at once. I am finished with you."

Her eyes widened in disbelief. "Finished with me? Why, you bastard!" She flew across the chamber, attacking him with her nails and fists.

He struck her hard across the cheek, sending her flying against a chair. She winced, touched her injured cheek, tears forming in her eyes. "You took my virginity and bedded me all these years. I was good enough for you in my youth, but now that I am older and unable to give you children, I cannot compare to the sweet, young bride who is fucking another. Think you she would want an old man with a small cock rather than a young, handsome knight who, from what I hear, has a large cock that could please any woman?"

He struck her again, furious at the images that raced through his mind. "Adelstan will pay dearly for his indiscretion."

"And what of your whore?"

"You were my whore, and a used-up whore at that." He lifted his chin high. "Rhiannon MacKay will be my wife, so you had best get used to it! In fact, I am done with you. Be gone from my sight, slut!"

TWENTY-THREE

Adelstan had left only minutes before Elspeth arrived with a wide smile on her face.

Rhiannon had not told her about Adelstan's visit, but as she nestled into bed, she listened while Elspeth gushed about Jorden.

"He is so lovely, Rhiannon."

"Aye, he is."

"Mmm," she said, a silly grin on her face as she cuddled closer to Rhiannon. "I wish I could take him with us."

"What if I told ye we did not have to leave?"

Elspeth's eyes narrowed. "What do ye mean?"

"Adelstan came to me tonight. He told me not to marry Malgor, that he wants me, and that he will take us from here. Aleysia is speaking to Renaud and hopefully all will be well."

"Oh, Rhiannon, I am so happy for ye." She hugged her tight.

Footsteps sounded outside her door, and a moment later a loud pounding followed.

Rhiannon and Elspeth looked at each other with raised brows.

"Open the door!"

Fear gripped Rhiannon's breast. "'Tis Malgor." Rhiannon scrambled from the bed, and slipped on her gown before she answered the door.

Malgor looked at Elspeth. "Leave us."

Elspeth glanced back at Rhiannon, who nodded. She was terrified to the very marrow of her bones. He was angry, and she knew without question that he had discovered the truth.

Malgor pushed Elspeth out the door, and Rhiannon had to bite her lip not to reprimand him for his rough treatment of her friend.

Malgor slammed the door behind him and threw the bolt into place without losing eye contact.

Steadying herself, Rhiannon looped her trembling fingers together behind her back, and lifted her chin. By damn she would not cower to this man. "To what do I owe this visit, my lord?"

"My lord, indeed," he said with a greasy smile. "I have it on good authority that my betrothed has been fucking another."

Rhiannon's stomach coiled tightly. His dark eyes narrowed into slits. "Tell me, did you have a man in your chamber this night?"

"Nay."

He laughed without mirth, his gaze shifting to the bed. "So innocent." For a large man, he moved fast, and was before her lifting her chin with rough fingers. "Someone is lying then, and I shall find out who it is."

She swallowed past the tightness in her throat.

"I am not a man who likes being betrayed, Rhiannon. I will

not tolerate it in my home, and I most certainly will not tolerate it in my marriage."

Biting the inside of her cheek in order to keep from saying what she yearned to, Rhiannon pulled away from him.

"Come back here," he said, grabbing her roughly, his fingers squeezing her upper arms.

Fear rushed along Rhiannon's spine as she looked into his cruel eyes. His face was red and sweaty, his eyes narrowed and dangerous. Dear Lord, would he kill her?

"Your father told me you wanted this marriage."

"Nay, I never wanted it."

He flinched as though she'd struck him.

"Am I not good enough for the fair Lady Rhiannon?" he asked, a malicious sneer on his lips. "You seduce another man, a most valuable soldier, and make me look the fool."

She looked him straight in the eye. "Ye flaunt your whore before me from the moment I set foot in Castle Almeron, and yet ye dare cast blame on me. What of your own actions, my lord?"

He slapped her so hard she fell back against the bed, knocking her head against the large post. Blood trickled from the cut near her temple, down the side of her cheek. "What do ye want of me, my lord? Why not marry the woman ye really love? I *want* ye to marry her."

"She is a commoner."

"But good enough to take to your bed each night." Rhiannon shook her head, wincing when pain shot through her skull.

"I am wedding you, Rhiannon, as soon as the priest is roused from his bed. Until then, you will stay here in this room, with me."

"I would rather die than marry ye."

His gaze shifted over her, his eyes glittering with lust. "You will be my bride, and know this . . . your lover will be sent far, far away from here. Indeed, once I tell King William what he has done, not even his brother-in-law can save him."

Though she tried not to show it, his words struck fear within her. She did not want to cause Adelstan any more grief, and she had no idea what King William would do once he learned of their affair.

"I will keep you locked in your chamber from the moment you open your eyes until the time you close them at night. I will touch you and use you in whatever way I so choose."

She slapped him hard against the face, and he instantly rallied with a backhand, sending her flying onto the floor. Before she could move, he was on her, his body flush to hers, his lips inches from hers.

He reached down to lift her skirts, his hands rough.

She screamed at the top of her lungs.

Malgor put a beefy hand over her mouth and reached under her kirtle again.

Dear God, he would rape her and there would be no one to save her.

She tried time and again to buck him off, and did her best to keep her thighs pressed tightly together, but he used his knees and brute strength to part them.

His small cock settled against her belly.

"You feel that, don't you? I like when you fight me."

That comment alone made her want to stop, but she didn't. She would submit when hell froze over.

He fumbled with his braies, and she screamed again. He clamped his hand tighter over her mouth, but she bit him.

"You bitch!" he cried, looking at his wounded hand before taking a handful of her hair in his meaty fist. He knocked her head back against the floor, hard.

A pounding started at the door.

"Hel—"

Malgor shifted just enough so she could try and lift her knee and maim him where it would do the most damage.

He clamped a hand around her throat. Blinded by the hair in her eyes, she clawed at his hand, but it was no use. She gritted her teeth when he reached beneath her skirts again.

Blackness lingered on the outer reaches of her mind. She heard voices and a cracking of wood, then she heard nothing at all.

Adelstan's chest heaved as the door crashed open and he saw Malgor straddling Rhiannon's limp body, his hands closed around her throat. A mixture of white-hot anger and fear shot through him and he was across the room, pulling de Cion off her. He slammed Malgor against the wall.

"Rhiannon!" Elspeth cried, going to her knees beside her limp body.

"You traitor," Malgor said, his breathing labored.

"What did you do to her?" Adelstan asked.

"What was coming. I will not be cuckolded by my betrothed."

"Does she live?" Adelstan asked Elspeth, almost afraid to hear the answer. Her face was ashen, and he could not see her chest rise and fall. "By God, if you killed her, you will not live to see the dawn."

"You dare threaten me?" de Cion taunted, wiping blood from his cheek where nail marks trailed down his face and neck. "You, the man who has been fucking my betrothed? You are as good as dead, Cawdor. What favor you have won from your brother-in-law will be ripped from you. You shall have nothing after King William finds out about this."

"You love another. Why not marry Jocelyn?"

"She is a whore, nothing less, nothing more. I've no more use for her."

Elspeth rested her ear on Rhiannon's chest. "She lives."

Relieved beyond measure, Adelstan said a silent prayer of thanks.

"Adelstan, her eyes are opening!"

Suddenly, someone pushed past him. The woman drew a dagger from her skirts and, with a mighty yell, thrust the blade into Malgor's chest.

A surprised de Cion looked at Jocelyn, his eyes wide in horror as he fell to his knees, blood spurting from the wound as he gasped for breath.

Adelstan went to Rhiannon and pulled her into his arms. She held him tight, her face pressed to his chest.

He brushed the hair off her forehead, furious to see the bruises there. "Malgor is dead. He can no longer harm you."

Jocelyn's wails filled the chamber. The woman, sick with grief, and with blood on her hands, sat against the wall, looking down at her dead lover in disbelief.

epilogue

Rhiannon floated on her back in the lake, looking up at the blue skies above her. She had found this place by chance one day when she and Adelstan had been out for a ride. The beauty of the setting had taken her breath away, nearly as much as the man whom she loved more than life.

He came up from the water, whipping his hair back out of his face as he pulled her to him. Her heart leapt to her throat as she looked at him, her legs wrapping around his lean waist. Her heart constricted with love for him, this handsome husband of hers.

Aye, husband. She could scarcely believe it, even now. That dark day so many weeks ago had faded, and since then, new memories had been made. Almeron Castle, along with Rhiannon's hand in marriage, had been given to Adelstan by Renaud, with King William's blessing. Everyone from Almeron had joined in the celebration, including Jocelyn, who was absolved of all charges relating to de Cion's murder.

Aleysia had wept through the entire wedding, Renaud holding her hand, his own eyes misting a bit as well. Neither sister nor brother-in-law had been ready for Adelstan to leave Braemere, but there had been no denying the happiness they had shared knowing he had fallen in love, and was starting a family of his own.

"I wonder if our child will be born with gills, wife," he said, a smile on his lips as a large hand cupped her rounded belly.

"Perhaps he will."

"Or she?"

Rhiannon smiled. "Aye, or she."

Adelstan's cock brushed against her heated core and she lifted a brow. "What if someone were to happen by and see us, my lord?"

"I do not care who would see us, my lady."

"Do ye not?"

"Nay, let the world know how much I desire my wife."

"Even though that wife be fat with child?"

His hands moved down her curves, over her bottom, dipping between the cleft there.

"You have never been so appealing to me as you are right now. In fact, the larger your belly grows, the more of you there is to love."

She tried to frown, but his words delighted her, for she knew he spoke the truth. He loved her, and she him, and she felt like the luckiest woman in the world.

"In fact, I shall show you just how very much I love you."

He slipped the head of his cock into her entrance and smiled innocently, leaving the work to her.

She slid down his length and sighed, biting her bottom lip as he touched her womb.

She would never tire of this, of these quiet moments, just the two of them. They had everything they could ever desire . . . a castle of their own, faithful friends, and a child on the way. The beginning of a wonderful life together.

His hands gripped her hips. Her fingernails grazed his shoulders, her body reaching closer to climax with each thrust, each solid stroke within her molten core.

Rhiannon looked into Adelstan's light eyes, and as her body quickened, she kissed him with all the love and intensity she felt, knowing she had truly found heaven on earth.